"Erica Olsen gives us the dream life of the Southwest in this striking collection, a landscape told in language as spare and pungent and exacting as the desert itself. A swift and lovely debut from a writer of real gifts."

—Kevin Canty, author of *Where the Money Went*

"These sly, heartbreaking stories capture the modern West, where the past is ever-present and the future is already here. The writing is clear and straightforward; but like the West itself, the stories are anything but simple. The characters are twenty-first-century wanderers, settlers, and adventurers who find, like those who came before them, that the West is a trickster, and the breathtaking view of the wide open spaces can be a fatal distraction from the rattler—or the bottomless canyon—in your path. Funny, grim stories from a writer with a sharp eye and a distinctive voice."

—Alison Baker, author of *How I Came West, and Why I Stayed*

"Beneath their polished surfaces, Erica Olsen's stories are subversive, sometimes darkly funny, and always disquieting. When you set off on a hike in her universe, be prepared for surprises. You may find yourself exploring Utah—or Norway—or a surreal faux wilderness where rainbows are regularly scheduled and gnats are outlawed. Also, prepare to be exhilarated. This accomplished writer really knows her way through the tricky zone between truth and falsehood where art is made."

—Susan Lowell Humphreys, author of *Ganado Red*

-------------------- Praise for *Recapture* --------------------

"A sharp, wise new voice from the American West, Erica Olsen is the real thing. As wild as David Foster Wallace or George Saunders and as tender as James Salter or Alice Munro, Olsen's stories are hilarious, painful, and achingly lovely. Whether conveying the lonesomeness of spending an evening in an Idaho hot spring loving the wrong person or envisioning a weird new world where a second Grand Canyon can be printed "grain by grain" from a 3D printer, Olsen is a joy to read."

—Amanda Eyre Ward, author of *Close Your Eyes*

"Like all good narratives, Erica Olsen's 'Grand Canyon II' suggests great consequence. The past is another country. The task of memory is impossible. No one exists and nothing ever happened. But somewhere in your brain, a beautiful lie is being spun...."

—Sarah Manguso, author of *The Guardians*

"*Recapture* is like a lost map of the backcountry, detailing the forgotten places where secrets shove up through the dust, pieces of lives demanding to be made whole. The territory is endlessly illuminating and constantly surprising, revealing a master storyteller at work."

—Kim Todd, author of *Tinkering with Eden: A Natural History of Exotic Species in America*

RECAPTURE
& OTHER STORIES

Erica Olsen

Torrey House Press, LLC
Utah

Some of the stories in this book have appeared in the following publications: "Grand Canyon II" in *Gulf Coast*; and, in different form, "Everything Is Red" in *Santa Monica Review*; "Driveaway" in *Terrain*; "Reverse Archaeology" in *ZYZZYVA*; "The Keepers" in *Tahoe Blues* (Bona Fide Books); "Going to Randsburg" in *Camas*; "Bristlecone" in *Blue Mesa Review*; "Everywhen" in *High Desert Journal*; "A Dish of Stinging Nettles" in *The Desert Voice* (Moab Poets & Writers).

"Anniversary Poem," by George Oppen, from *New Collected Poems,* copyright © 1972 by George Oppen. Reprinted by permission of New Directions Publishing Corp.

Utah: A Guide to the State, compiled by Workers of the Writers' Program of the Work Projects Administration for the State of Utah. Copyright © 1941 by Utah State Institute of Fine Arts.

First Torrey House Press Edition, October 2012
Copyright © 2012 by Erica Olsen

Published by Torrey House Press, LLC
P.O. Box 750196
Torrey, Utah 84775 U.S.A.
http://torreyhouse.com

International Standard Book Number: 978-1-937226-05-3
Library of Congress Control Number: 2012938795

Author photo: Michael Troutman/www.dmtimaging.com © D. M. Troutman
Cover and book design by Jeff Fuller http://shelfish.weebly.com

RECAPTURE
& OTHER STORIES

CONTENTS

We are troubled by incredulity
We are troubled by scratched things

—George Oppen

Everything is red.

—*Utah: A Guide to the State*
Compiled by Workers of the Writers'
Program of the Work Projects
Administration for the State of Utah

GRAND CANYON II

For a long time I wanted to go back to the Grand Canyon. Then came the dual catastrophe: an earthquake that left Grand Canyon Village in ruins, and a mining accident, the details of which have never been released to the public. So, it's too late. No one knows how long the decontamination will take. A visitor center and replica canyon off Interstate 40 near Williams, Arizona, had long been proposed as a way to relieve stress on park resources; after the disaster, those plans were revived and Grand Canyon II was approved and constructed. The new park replicates the five-mile stretch that historically drew the most visitors, from Grand Canyon Village to Yaki Point, encompassing the main overlooks and the Bright Angel and South Kaibab trailheads. It is a geological clone made possible by the recent advances in rapid prototyping with which we have all become familiar. Using technology similar to that developed for bioprinting organs for transplant, Grand Canyon II was printed in 3D by depositing layers of igneous, metamorphic, and sedimentary rock, from the inner gorge to the upper

canyon, from Vishnu schist to the Kaibab formation.
Grain by grain, the canyon was remade. In an office
in Los Angeles, I worked on the editorial team, checking contours, textures, Munsell color specifications.
I proofread the Coconino sandstone. The design files
replicated native plants, the effects of erosion, marine
fossils, even graffiti and the scars from mule shoes
and trekking poles. Birds and animals find their own
way in: flickers, hummingbirds, a thriving population
of Abert's squirrels, the omnipresent mule deer. After the first few hundred feet, depth is an illusion. The
river is waterless. These compromises were found ac-
ceptable by most visitors.

My parents took me to the Grand Canyon, the
original, in 1970, when I was five years old. It was
the first and only time my Norwegian and Korean
grandparents met. Years later, looking at that ritual
of American astonishment (for my generation, Kodak
is the color of the past itself), I can't help but see the
diminishment of our lives. The now curled and lonesome snapshot reveals something deceptive, essen-
tially untrue, about the scene, the big promise at our
backs. They didn't travel. In me there must have been,
already, the promise of unsuitable boyfriends. But for
a long time I wanted to go back to the Grand Canyon,
though it's not clear to me if it was a dream, an obliga-
tion, or some less easily defined but no less pressing
need. In any case, it's the new park that I pay to enter.
The crowds are busy with cameras and views. I fill my

lungs with ponderosa-scented air. I brush away a fly.

Did you think for some reason I wouldn't be taken in? Would you believe that being here pierces me like an artifact of my own memory? At the edge of this vast and unimaginable copy, I remember tent-shade and fire-warmth. I reach for absent hands.

ADVENTURE HIGHWAY

the approach to Moab from the south: the gigantic earth was Gulliver, strapped down by the grid of roadways and power lines. The mighty red rock suddenly hamstrung, all knees and knuckles. Tyler Swanson was driving in high dudgeon. Lately, dudgeon had become Swanson's mode of being, though he tried to keep it at a low-to-moderate level. Not today. What had happened to Moab? It seemed all motels. On the north side of town, on the way up to Arches, he noticed people pedaling their bikes earnestly on a path that paralleled the highway on the east. If the path had been there before, and he didn't think it had been, it certainly didn't used to be paved. What had happened to dirt?

That ribbon of asphalt—it symbolized all that was wrong with the world. An ever-expanding list that included, among recent items:

> Having been passed over for a job that should by rights have been his
> Having to go on this trip without his girlfriend, Courtney

Swanson had a feeling that things in general had been made easier for people in general, but not for him. Regarding the latter item: Courtney had canceled literally at the last minute, as he was loading gear into the car. One moment he was cheerfully wrangling tarps and lawn chairs, the next her voice was buzzing into his ear the excuse that work was "crazy busy."

He should go, she'd said—of course he should go.

And so he did, resolving to make the best of it. This time, this gift, this Swanson solitaire.

For solitude, Moab in April was, it seemed, exactly the wrong place. The presence of so many determined fun-havers was giving Swanson a jaundiced view of canyon country. Sweating in his vehicle, he waited his turn through the Arches entrance station. Through his lenses (amber, polarized) the heaps of rock looked like so much hamburger. He parked next to a planted island, which a spindly cottonwood shared with some bravely blooming globemallow. On the other side of the parking lot some people were taking photos of the cliffs adjacent to their RV. Maybe this was as far as they were planning to go. To the west, the cliff wall amplified the sound of traffic where the highway climbed out of town. Swanson heard the other inescapable sound, the confirming horn-honk of a car door locking, and groaned.

He'd wanted an adventure, or at least a getaway from the Bay Area winter of endless rain, but he struggled through the new visitor center. The building was very nice, depressingly nice, with its displays of faux sandstone, its lessons on the Entrada and Chinle formations and all the rest. A video screen set into an indoor cliff told Swanson *Congratulations!* He didn't want to know what for. He missed old visitor centers with their quaint dioramas, their dusty specimens of taxidermy and such. The high-gloss treatment here was like a billboard for the real world, which needed no advertisement. It was right there! Out the window! Through the glass, the red cliffs shimmered, a little paler than they were in reality. Inside was a scaled-down version of Delicate Arch that Swanson didn't want to walk through and yet there he was, walking through it. If the outside was hamburger, this sandstone mockup was pink slime, the processed beef that had been so much in the news lately. An indictment of our culture, Swanson thought.

What worried him most was just how many things seemed to him, these days, to be an indictment of our culture. He understood this for what it was, a sign he was middle-aged. Moab, at this time of year, was a veritable slide show of past and present fun he'd inexplicably missed out on.

For him there was the parking lot ordeal of sun block and sun hat and sun shirt.

He drove up the switchbacks of the escarpment, passing the *Gather No Wood in Park* road sign, whose medieval diction he used to alter to *Gather Ye*, then rhetorically inquire, *What about wool? Is wool-gathering allowed?* He passed it with a morose acknowledgment; there was something that used to make him smile.

At the trailhead Swanson overheard a vacation dad lecturing his vacation son, who was maybe nine years old: *When are you going to start acting appropriately?* Which, in context, may well have been a reasonable question, but Swanson glared at the dad, felt for the kid.

He felt for himself, having planned this trip buoyantly for months. But to face facts: Courtney had been questioning the travel arrangements. He'd proposed car camping—air mattresses and bathrooms, with plumbing whenever possible. Her reaction had been less than enthusiastic. He had to admit, now, she'd been giving him signals that she didn't want to go. She was really more of a hotel girl.

He passed a geology class trip from somewhere ridiculously far away, Texas or Tennessee, giving a group thumbs-up to some roadside rock formation.

Spring break.

Swanson headed down the Park Avenue trail then ducked off it at Courthouse Wash. The academic year had not been good to him. He'd put in the time as an adjunct—freshman English, American Studies. Swanson had always been flexible, accommodating— and he had not been selected for an interview. That was a blow. He suspected his colleagues of looking askance at his methodology. His ecocriticism. Swanson had not published, not enough and not well enough; he'd put himself on the fast track to perishing. But he wasn't dead yet! He wanted—he wanted—what? Utah, the geologic opera that used to make what he called (for lack of a better word) his soul feel as big and light as a balloon, wasn't working for him this time. He looked at nature, and he felt nothing. Maybe it happened to everyone. Up the wash, where he'd hoped for tranquility, some boorish idiots, or idiotic boors—no doubt the same ones who'd let their kids scratch their names and the date across the rock of the main trail—were hallooing for the echo.

He hadn't seen her for a few weeks, between his grading and her work schedule. That might mean something. Or nothing—people were busy sometimes. There had been a fight, though. He remembered her angry tears, the queasy feeling that still came over him when he recalled her revelation that she didn't want to settle. He hated that word, settle.

"Settle down?" he'd asked.

"Settle." She added, "It's not fair to *you*."

Yelling and clapping. Were they playing Marco Polo back there?

Swanson slunk away, continued on to the next pullout.

Where, next to an interpretive sign, a ranger was lecturing someone about hiking off trail. The trail itself was quilted with footprints. In his sun-blocking armor, Swanson plodded past a plethora of petrified hoopla.

And then, just like that, he'd had enough.

Enough! he said to himself.

He stuffed the hated nylon sombrero into a trash can and marched himself back to the car.

Before getting on the road he checked for a signal, checked for messages (he had none), then speed-dialed Courtney. He got voicemail. "Hey. It's Tyler," he said. "I was just. I was just wondering." He laughed a little laugh. "When are you going to start acting appropriately?"

South of Moab, he was back in starkly empty country, the sage plain interrupted here and there by reefs and fins of exposed rock. Back before it was paved, this road was one of the country's last adventure highways. He'd read that somewhere. That was before his time, of course, but adventure highway was what he wanted. Spaced out on open space, miles and miles of it, he almost missed the turn lane. He braked hard and without signaling swung right onto the turn-off to Newspaper Rock. The RV behind him sounded a bitchy toot of the horn. Swanson wished his fellow humans a fuck-you-very-much. This was exhilarating. Up ahead was a good pullout, with a sturdy pinyon-juniper grove for shade. He set off cross-country in a tonic rage—the ranger the trail the rules—then headed up a pink sand wash.

Out here, he could begin to face facts. What mattered here was life and death, rock and rainfall, the weird-looking cryptogamic crust that Swanson stepped considerately around. Not the romantic travails of a forty-year-old, the humiliation of another middle-aged breakup. Courtney was a few years older than he was, and in the back of his mind he'd assumed that when things went south it would be his doing. (A pretty grad student, a conference fling.) He'd been wrong about that. In her forties, Courtney had started to turn heads. And she was likely not to be there when he returned. She'd said as much the last time they got together, after the holidays. He just hadn't wanted to hear it. The thousand-mile drive had given him ample time to turn her words into something ambiguous, something he could reasonably interpret in his favor.

He hiked hard, feet plowing the thick hot sand, until the voice in his mind quieted and he started to see what was around him, the beautiful world. A phalanx of cliffs glittering through his sunglasses, some unassuming low-growing yellow flowers. *Goosefoot*, he thought; the name came unbidden from some store of knowledge he'd forgotten he had. Feeling heavy, weary, he paused for water and a snack, then gave in to the gravitational tug of the earth. He sat himself down on some Late Triassic. (In relation to Swanson's ability to identify strata, the visitor center had done its work.) A weatherbeaten juniper extended its limbs in fellowship. Some Mormon tea was growing in its shadow, gaunt yet luxuriant.

He stretched himself out on a bench of warm rock for a nap a collared lizard would envy.

He woke up in near-dark, shivering, and the water bottle had rolled away somewhere, and Swanson, who had wanted an adventure, cursed his stupidity.

How far in had he hiked? An hour or two, surely no more than that. Though there may have been some wandering near the end, some wandering concurrent with poetic musings and observings, during which time he may not have paid strict attention to his surroundings. During the time he took to assess the situation the last light vanished from the sky. He was in his technical shorts with the mesh vented panels, and the breeze rattled him. Why hadn't he worn pants? He blinked against the confusing darkness.

His headlamp, of course, was in his car. (He remembered how this trip began, his pride in packing the gear just so. Once he'd gotten on the road it was a mess, of course, his good work undone. Why had he tried so hard in the first place?) The car was at the trailhead, and the trailhead—he did not know where it was.

He fumbled for his cell phone. He could use it to light his way.

He scanned the ground, gray and indistinct, for his own footprints, instructing himself: Don't fall. That was the first rule of hiking, day or night. Swanson set his feet deliberately. Why had he worn sandals? They were like huge flopping rafts, ill-fitting, a stupid choice. His feet chafed, and almost certainly he had blisters. No, the first rule of hiking was Be Not Stupid, and he was violating it by hiking in the dark instead of waiting for daylight. Or waiting for rescue. Not that he needed rescuing. And if he did, how embarrassing would it be to be rescued while wearing technical shorts? He should never have let himself buy them.

Swanson trod stone and sand and cobbles, watchful, mindful of his limitations.

Soon enough, his eyes grew accustomed to the night. The bare rock reflected starlight. The night was full of strangeness. He heard a bird he didn't know. Once he jumped at the appearance of a huge beetle that hovered in the air at knee level, clacking and swaying like some miniature robot drone. He had no idea where in the sky the moon would appear or in what phase it would be, but maybe if the world could pave a bike path from Moab to Arches it could give Swanson the moon. Swanson was not one acquainted with the night but it was remarkably freeing to stride along like this, unhoused. If he'd thought to stick a fleece into his daypack he was sure he could have ridden out the night in comfort. Why had he never taken up backpacking? This was the West, the wild and the free, the unfettered and confident. "You make a left turn at Albuquerque," he proclaimed in the voice of Bugs Bunny.

Swanson fell.

Climbing up a small ledge he was pretty sure he'd descended on his way in, his sandaled foot slipped. He lost his balance and sat back in the air, landing awkwardly on his shoulders on the downslope, legs pedaling. *Bassackwards* was the word for it. It took a few tries before he succeeded in righting himself. Sand and juniper bits in his hair and down his shirt collar. He brushed himself off hurriedly, as if there were an audience to witness his ineptitude and discomfiture and so on. He felt for blood, found his phone, calmed his racing heart.

It was not the end of Swanson.

And then the moon, the kindly moon, came up and saved him, kept him from continuing up the ledge into God knows where. In the moonlight he could see his footprints waffling down the sandy wash—the sandals were new and the tread was clear. He followed them. After an easy walk, he saw the glint of moon on metal: his car.

How long until the car would have been noticed—until he was missed? Swanson felt weepy and indignant. Nobody cared where he was. He drove too fast, crossing the center line on the curves. Once he almost hit a rabbit as it raced in furred desperation across the roadway.

Single and forty, survivor of various ordeals, he turned back onto 191.

Monticello was a scatter of lights, the promise of a meal and a motel, civilization. Swanson felt suddenly, absurdly at home. He'd been there before. Monti*cello* as in cellophane, he thought; not *cello* like the instrument or Thomas Jefferson's house. He could see lights high up on the mountain road, someone else making the long drive into town. Hart's Draw Road, it was called. The bloom of memory seemed wondrous to Swanson, as transient and lovely as spring itself. He slowed to forty-five, and saw the Maverik station on the north side of town.

Where the heck did that *come from?* he thought. It had not been there on his way up just two days before. Lights and angels and restrooms.

He pulled in across an admirably smooth curb cut, parked next to a full-size pickup with Arizona plates. The Maverik was obviously brand new, its expanses of red and black graphic and unspoiled. It was like a child's toy just out of the package, life-size and dazzling. The asphalt was unmarked with wads of gum or sticky pools of spilled diesel. The pumps were a remarkable lineup, newly extruded from the plastic Eden machine and barely touched by human hands.

Swanson went in and found the restroom. He had never imagined that a gas station bathroom could be so pristine. It was a wonder.

In the mirror over the sink he found that he looked no better and no worse than anyone else.

The pickup pulled out while he was in the restroom, leaving Swanson the only customer in the store. He wandered the aisles. He admired the photo murals of mountains and canyons and the disembodied portion of spruce tree and the dummy kayaker suspended in midair. He admired the taxidermy. At the sandwich trough, the choice between turkey and Black Forest ham brought tears to his eyes. He picked up one of each. He picked up potato chips and tortilla chips and honey-roasted cashew nuts and a pickle in a vacuum-sealed bag with a picture of a cartoon pickle on it. He did not stumble, and no one knew what he'd been through.

At the register, he ventured a mild flirtation with the checkout girl. Jolted out of her reverie, she blinked at him in astonishment and wished him a nice day.

Swanson went out to pump his gas. From where he was standing, under the canopy, he could just make out the poster on the video rental kiosk—some movie in which attractive people met, then fell in love. All eyes and lips and hair, and a title whose lettering, at this distance, he couldn't read. He made up his own title. *Maverik: A Love Story*. For the first time in a long time he felt that it wouldn't hurt him to watch something like that.

EVERYTHING IS RED

I was walking over to the trading post to see Barbara, the trader's wife. That morning, opening a can of peaches, I'd sliced into the palm of my left hand. The cut was deep, and close enough to the wrist to scare me a little.

The trading post stood at the bottom of a rough road that dipped down into a canyon. It was a small stone building in the lee of the cliffs, shaded by big cottonwoods. A car I didn't know was out in front.

There were two men inside the trading post. One was the archaeologist whose camp was down the road from mine. I knew the other man by sight—one of the newspaper reporters come out from Denver to cover the Indian war. The reporter was sitting by the stove, drinking coffee and eating Barbara's biscuits. His flannel suit was wrinkled, and some letters stuck out of the breast pocket. A red and yellow serape was draped around one shoulder and trailed down to the floor.

I thought there was an Indian too, one of the archaeologist's mummies waiting to be wrapped in newspaper, packed in a crate, and shipped back to the museum in Chicago. It looked like the ones I'd seen before, sitting head to knees in the dim corner. But then my eyes adjusted to the light, and I saw that it was only some sacks of flour and a rug draped over the top.

The post carried groceries and hardware, blankets and tack. Baskets were propped on some of the shelves. Behind the counter, strings of silver and turquoise were bunched together, waiting to be redeemed. Dust was thick on some of the tags. Only a small part of it was dead pawn. Navajo rugs were laid across the counters and stacked on the floor against one wall. You could smell the grass the baskets were made of, and the smell of sheep was in the rugs. Set back on one shelf was a splendid black and white olla, an old cliff dweller jar.

The trader was away in Flagstaff but his spirit was everywhere—behind the counter, and in the lingering odor of his tobacco, and the creak of floorboards weighted by years of his footfall.

The trader's wife was a tall woman with short brown hair fluffed into a wave. She unwound the cloth off my hand—I'd wrapped a piece of old shirt around it. Barbara had been a nurse before her marriage.

"How did you manage this?" she asked.

"Pure carelessness," I said.

The men came close to look at the wound.

"He'll need stitches," the archaeologist said. He turned his own hand palm up and examined it in sympathy.

"I'll get my bag." The trader's wife went into the other room.

The reporter said, "When I was starting out at the *Times*, I knew a guy who was bit by a rattlesnake."

The "war" was over, Paiute Posey was dead, and the streets of Bluff and Blanding were safe again for whites. But the sight of my blood made his eyes go bright with excitement.

> > < <

The trader's wife came out of the back room with a doctor's bag. She took some things out—antiseptic, a proper bandage. Her dress was printed with flowers. On her feet were men's boots. I'd seen her wear city shoes with heels when she was getting ready to drive down to Flag herself.

The archaeologist was pacing the bullpen in a scholarly manner, with his hands clasped behind his back. From time to time he cut his eyes toward the olla. It was something over a foot high and round as a pumpkin, but with a flaring neck wider than a pumpkin's stem, and two tiny handles low on the sides. Except for a band of white from the base to the handles, it was painted all over with zigzag bands of black. Whoever made it, they'd had a steady hand.

"I saw Burnett last week," the archaeologist said.

"How is Jim?" the trader's wife asked.

"He won't sell."

"Won't he?" The trader's wife poured hot water from the kettle into a pan.

The olla belonged to Jim Burnett, a rancher, and he kept it at the trading post. He said he was afraid of it getting broken out at his place.

"I was after him all last year for that olla," the archaeologist said. "I offered him ten dollars. He wouldn't take it."

The trader's wife smiled. "Maybe he knows it's worth more." She added some wood to the stove.

Burnett had found that pot on his land, rim and shoulders exposed after a late summer rain.

All over Utah, the pots were unburying themselves.

> > < <

When the fire was crackling, the reporter addressed the room in general. "I've been up at Posey's grave."

Leaning up against the counter, the archaeologist shifted and cleared his throat.

"As a matter of fact, I went up there twice," the reporter said.

The trader's wife lowered the pan of hot water onto the table. She drew a chair up next to me.

To the reporter, she said, "Did you see the grave?"

"Well, yes, I did. That's one good Indian." The reporter waited for someone to laugh, but no one did. "We went up there after the marshal left. The marshal told us Posey was dead, but he wouldn't say where he buried him. He promised the Indians he wouldn't tell. But the men in town—they wanted proof."

"He was shot, wasn't he?" asked the trader's wife. She washed my hand. With the blood gone, the cut didn't look as bad. It was deep, but it looked clean.

"Shot in the leg, at the start of the war," the reporter said. "Blood poisoning got him."

"War?" the archaeologist broke in. "I wouldn't call some stolen cattle and a shoot-out a war."

The reporter shrugged. "The marshal left a plain trail all the way up Comb Wash. There was a photographer with us. He got his photos and then we buried him again. Decently.

"A couple of days later, the Indian agent wants to go out and see for himself, so we take him up there and he gets his portrait with old Posey too."

The trader's wife said, "It's a shame he couldn't rest in peace."

"It's more than a shame," the archaeologist said. "It's criminal."

"What's criminal? Digging up Indians?" The reporter gathered up the ends of his serape. "I hear you've dug up one or two yourself."

The archaeologist stiffened. "The circumstances are entirely different. My work—"

"Hush now," the trader's wife said. "I'm trying to fix up this hand." She unstoppered a bottle, and I winced at the smell of Mercurochrome.

The archaeologist had taken a step toward the reporter. "The marshal will hear about this," he said.

"Why don't you tell him?" The reporter laughed.

His eyes went to the pretty olla on the shelf. "Is that for your museum or for your collection? I've seen what you do," he said.

I've seen him too—him and his wife. A savory blue smoke comes from their camp. Behind it is the smell of the earth, sweet iron and rust and snow. The low, brush-covered mounds are pregnant with artifacts. The painted kivas lift their skirts.

The trader's wife set the bottle of antiseptic down. She held up a hand to the archaeologist. Then she eyed the reporter. "You've got your mail," she said, pointedly.

"I was just leaving," he said.

> > < <

The door dropped shut. We heard the car start. The trader's wife put some gauze over my palm and pressed my other hand hard on top of it.

The archaeologist resumed his pacing. When the trader's wife went to the counter where she had left the bag with the surgical needles and the thread, he asked, "How much does Burnett owe on his account?"

The book was open on the counter. The trader's wife glanced at it.

"Twenty-two dollars and sixty cents," she said.

The archaeologist reached into his pocket.

"Call it twenty-three even," he said and laid the money on the counter. "I want that pot."

She sighed. "All right," she said. "But if Burnett takes it up with you—"

"I'll be responsible," he said.

He let himself behind the counter and took down the pot. He embraced it tenderly as he shouldered the door open. The bright sun knifed into the room. Motes of dust rose and fell around him, and there was a shock of green from the cottonwood leaves.

> > < <

For the second time that morning I watched her monitor the closing of the door. At the sound of the catch she gave a little nod—whether of satisfaction or resignation, I couldn't say. To my ear, the scrape of wood on wood suggested something conjugal.

She gave me the same kind of long, measured look she'd just given the door. Measuring me—as if to ask what I'd have done in all these circumstances—or maybe just measuring the distance between us.

The wood hissed in the stove, and the floorboards creaked, and I looked away.

The trader's wife said, "There weren't any letters for you this week."

"I figured there weren't," I said. "I figured you would have said if there were." I said, "That's all right, Barb."

"Still," she said. "I should have mentioned it, earlier. I should have said."

I'd come out to Utah with the oil company in '21 and stayed on to do some prospecting myself. I set up camp a mile or so from the river. Later, I built a little house, a dugout, one room, that stayed warm and dry all winter. Next door to the dugout, I devised a root cellar. They looked fine, the root cellar and the dugout.

My wife was back in California all that time. Most of the letters I'd ever gotten in my life, and all the best ones, had come from her. But there hadn't been a letter in a while. That was the day I stopped asking for one, the day I had my first clumsy thoughts about what else in life a man might want.

Down by the San Juan there's a layer of limestone made up entirely of tiny shells. There's a place where oil flows straight out of the rock into the river. Everything is red. The rocks, and the soil, and the thick fast-moving water in the river.

The trader's wife resumed her work on my hand. The slim needle nipped—ten, twelve times. The ends of the threads floated up like spider's silk. She took away the soaked pad of gauze and put down another. She wrapped a clean bandage around my wrist and across my palm and between my thumb and fingers.

"There," she said. "There."

Her hands were warm. They held mine for a moment. Under the bandages, I could feel the wet gauze, the blood still flowing.

DRIVEAWAY

On certain days in the city, a golden smog filtered through the streets, a kind of pollen falling on our upturned faces. I'd get glimpses—the crispness of possibility, the vitamin smell of a new twenty-dollar bill.

> > < <

Derelicts stood around on the sidewalk in front of the Basque hotel. It was part of my job to escort them off the steps. Looking at them was like looking back into the last century. These men were daguerreotypes. They didn't know what a city was doing around them. There was one with a magnificent head of hair and a curled white beard. He looked like the mountain man in the painting, all brown and gold, that hung in the old library before the renovation. His canvas clothes had stiffened into a kind of leather, and his eyes remembered the endless views from the high passes where snow doesn't melt.

It was the other ones I was afraid of, the ones dressed normal. Get up close to them and it was *fucker,*

fucker, fucker, walking fast down Market Street, or on the bus.

The homeless! Under my window, they worked for hours lettering their cardboard signs, while discussing the Bible in amiable voices. "Did you hear about the tower of Babel?" One of them posed this question to the other. It was news.

This was in San Francisco in 1999. I'd left Salt Lake without my belongings. At the Catholic thrift shops on Sutter I'd found some shirts and pants in my size, and a pair of shoes that were still shaped like someone else's feet. Only later did it occur to me that these clothes had probably belonged to some young man who had died, and I was walking around the city dressed as his ghost.

> > < <

In April the snow, I knew, would be melting from the mesa tops. I went looking for Prine, who I thought might be willing to drive me back to Utah.

I'd found a site, the previous autumn, in a little side canyon past the long house on the mesa. The floor of the alcove was already all dug up. Some of those holes were a hundred years old. The ruins were tumbled over. But the late summer rains loosened things up, and the artifacts—some baskets and a cache of unfinished sandals—were popping out of the ground.

My friends had gone back to the long house with a backhoe, and that's how they got caught. They implicated me, but for lack of evidence, I was let go with a fine and a five-hundred-word essay on how what I'd done was wrong.

All this time, I'd been carrying around some Polaroids of what I'd found. I liked to think about the money I could make, just by going back.

> > < <

Prine was out at Ocean Beach, watching over his rods—five of them planted in the black, oily sand. He used to work for the airlines, until he hurt his back. Now he spent his days at the beach, here in the city, or down in Pacifica, fishing for salmon.

He shook his head in a mournful way. "That car," he said. "I've got it parked somewhere. I'm having trouble with it."

I was embarrassed to ask outright, but I was hoping he would give me the money for a bus ticket.

"Let me see those pictures again," he said.

I fanned out my Polaroids. Nothing was the slightest bit frayed or eaten away. For Basketmaker artifacts that was as good as it got.

"I'll come with you, but I'm not getting involved in anything illegal." He wanted some assurance.

"It's all public land," I told him.

"We'll go, and then we'll come right back," he agreed.

"It won't take more than three or four days." I could hardly believe I'd succeeded in devising a workable plan. What a beautiful vision I had, then, of these shores, the gentle licking of the green waves, and myself far from here. There was hope.

Then I remembered. "How are we going to get there?"

"A car will be the least of our problems," Prine said.

> > < <

We got off the Samtrans bus down past the airport, where the driveaway places were.

"Which one of you is the driver?" the man at the counter asked.

"He is," I said.

"I am." Prine confirmed it.

"Do you have a reference?" the man asked. "Someone who can vouch for your character?"

"That would be me," I said.

"How long have you known the driver?" the manager asked me.

"I don't know. Eight, nine years." I had to think.

"Relationship?"

"He's my brother-in-law." The ease of this testimony surprised me, as if I'd opened my mouth and fluent Dutch came out. Lynne wasn't my wife anymore, but he was her brother.

We signed the paper for our car—a white Saab just a few years old, belonging to a marketing manager who was being transferred to Salt Lake. Out of the printer came a sheet of directions to the drop-off point in West Jordan.

That was all there was to it! I had to laugh. In my mind we were all over the country in this car.

"There's something I want to know. Why doesn't everyone do this?" I asked, as we were driving out of the city.

"Most people don't have the imagination."

I did. In the canyon, it was likely we'd find a burial, with jewelry—shell beads and bracelets.

We were driving the Emigrant Trail backwards, reverse pioneers. The discards were everywhere, on the side of the road. All we had to do was gather them up.

In Winnemucca, the fast-food restaurants and motels had been built right up to the edges of the cemetery, surrounding the graves. That's probably how it was in the mining camps.

"Do you want me to drive?" I asked. We'd stopped for gas.

"That's all right," Prine said.

"Well, I can drive if you want me to. There's nothing wrong with my eyes." I was taking some medicine to help me pay attention, and also, I'd finally gotten around to keeping a list of things I needed to do, as a high school counselor had once suggested.

But he didn't want me to. So, until it got dark, I worked puzzles out of a book I found under the seat— mazes and jumbles, where you rearrange the letters to answer the question in the little cartoon. There weren't any surprises on the road. Just nightfall—the sky pressing down.

> > < <

I remembered a time from my boyhood, camping with a group from church, under mountainsides so high it seemed like someone must have built them, like they were dams holding something back. At night, through the tent walls, I felt them towering.

It was the same way with this drive. The invisible world was made visible, as we came into Salt Lake, with the mountains on one side, the desert on the other, the lights of the hotels, and the wide, empty streets after midnight.

"We'll need shovels," I said as we passed a shopping center surrounded by acres of parking lot.

"I've already thought of that," Prine said.

In the suburbs south of the city, he pulled up outside a little house with a swingset on one side, and a tricycle and some toy vehicles overturned on the lawn. The television was chattering inside. After we'd been stopped there a minute, the porch light went on.

"I'm just going in for a second," Prine said. "You don't have to come in if you don't want to."

"Where are we?" I asked.

"I'll just run in to get Cody," Prine said.

This was Lynne's house, then. Cody was her stepson, one of her new husband's kids.

"Oh, I'm coming in," I said.

Cody was in the kitchen, spreading peanut butter on bread and putting sandwiches in plastic bags. A backpack leaned against the wall just inside the door.

Prine looked him over. "I forgot you don't eat meat," he observed.

Cody waggled one foot at him. He was wearing canvas sneakers. "No animal products," he said.

When I pulled out my cigarettes he caught my eye and held it. He was one of those kids.

"I'll just go outside, then," I said. But I didn't.

"You could've told me he was coming," Cody said to Prine. He had small eyes and a chin beard that stuck out, and he didn't stand up straight. But I couldn't think of what to say to him yet.

House sounds in a dim room, water running in the sink. The TV surged with tearful late-night music, and outside in the dark, a bird was singing its song. These sounds comforted me. None of them was my fault. I lay back on the loveseat at one end of the kitchen, where the table ought to be, while Prine and Cody went about the house gathering up supplies.

"Hey." Prine shook me awake.

Lynne was there.

"Bill's going to be home soon," she said. She was in her nightgown, a plain white thing with ribbon woven in and out around the edges. She was putting things away while she talked, the way women who have children are always doing. I looked at her knees, and then at her hair, a straight, shining wall keeping me out.

She looked at her brother. "You, I'd expect this from," she told him.

Prine had two shovels in his hands, from the garage.

I swallowed. My throat felt raw. I had a cold that I couldn't get rid of, but this wasn't one of my symptoms. I wanted to be touched under my clothes. It had been a long time, and I'd have given anything for that. "You loved me, and then you didn't." Did I actually speak or only think it? She was looking at me the way a snake might look at the skin it sheds.

But I was seeing her in her nightgown, and then, in my mind, her wedding dress, stiff with lace, a kind of coral encrusted on her body. And then the shroud, but I wouldn't be around to bury her. The heat of love was streaming out of me. Then, like someone suffering from hypothermia, I didn't feel the cold any more. I could take off all of my clothes. I could lie down in the snow.

"You waltz in here," she said. In her hands, at that moment, she was holding a yellow dump truck. She looked older than when I knew her. I was sure I looked exactly the same.

> > < <

Cody put out his hand, and Prine gave him the keys. So I guess he was old enough to drive—fifteen or sixteen.

She came out in front of the house to see us go. She'd put a sweater, a blue cardigan, over her shoulders, and the sleeves hung down over her arms. She shrugged the front of the sweater together, with one hand, as we backed out of the driveway. That gesture went into the part of my brain that knows indisputable facts. State capitals, which planet has the rings.

We drove through the night, through Spanish Fork and Helper and Price. Then we were in the canyon country, filling up at an all-night station outside of Green River. The big trucks coursed by, hauling away the dead, and dragging the sun into place for another day.

"Cody. How'd you get a name like that?" I said when he got back in the car.

He shook his head. "What?"

"You're too old to be a Cody." The West was being overrun with four- and five-year-old Codys, Tanners, and Tylers. He was one of them, but older. I stared at the back of his head. He could have been my son.

Prine was asleep in the passenger seat, and later on, Cody also nodded off. His foot was still on the gas, although the car slowed down, eventually floating onto the shoulder. We continued to move forward while the canyon walls grew tall around us, like something we were dreaming.

"What? What?" Prine was talking in his sleep, answering his dreams.

I opened my eyes. "Is it a flash flood?" A roaring sound was all around us, like you'd imagine boulders would make crashing against each other. The car filled with light like an egg about to hatch. The earth was coming up with the sun. We got out and stomped around on the hard, frosty ground. Somehow we had steered off the road right up into a beautiful valley.

Everything was red—the rock spires, and the ground, and the bottoms of the silky clouds.

"Do you hear that?" I asked them. Was this a sound that always accompanied the sunrise, and we just couldn't hear it in the city with all the traffic and the power lines? It came from behind the rocks, then rose up over our heads.

"Well, would you look at that," Prine said.

A helicopter was hovering, with a truck slung on ropes underneath, settling onto the flat top of one of the red buttes.

"So that's how they do it," Prine said.

"They could do it with computers, but they're doing it for real," I marveled.

We felt like we were watching a man land on the moon, the small rockets lowering onto the remote surface. We were witnesses.

> > < <

After that, it felt almost like an afterthought to go up on the mesa. The road climbed, and the rest of the world dropped away. We passed, rusted on a ledge, the uranium truck that had gone over in the fifties. Then we were a thousand feet higher, in the pinyon and juniper forest. It was colder up there, and patches of old snow lingered under the trees.

Prine was at the wheel. I sat forward, watching for the mile markers at the side of the highway.

"Slow down, slow down," I said.

"There's supposed to be a road here?" Prine said.

"There is," I said. "Turn. *Here*."

It was just a wide spot between the trees, until we nosed down into the gully and up the other side. Tracks appeared, leading into the forest.

"*Wunderbar*," Prine said, easing the car between the trees.

"What about rangers?" Cody asked.

"No one comes up here but Navajos cutting wood." I was excited about the burial I was sure we would find.

Brush was dragging on the sides of the marketing manager's car. At a clearing, Prine backed up into the trees. There were soda cans lying around on the ground, the lettering bleached off, and yellow plastic jugs where Indians had changed their oil. Tire tracks went everywhere, in overlapping figure eights. We set off on foot down one of the two-tracks. I wouldn't have been surprised to come upon a little hut, a woodcutter's or a witch's, someone who knew our names and what we were doing there.

The mesa was thick with pinyon and widebranched juniper. Between the trees there were deep, soft gullies that we plunge-stepped down. In a little while, we came to the white rimrock and dropped down into the canyon.

I knew where I was. The big overhang. The ledge, with the tiny corncobs and the pottery that hikers had laid out on the rocks. There were two and a half small rooms still standing, and pits dug out all along the back where the other rooms had been. The

Basketmaker level was underneath those.

"Okay," Cody said. "Let's get to work."

Prine took hold of a shovel.

"What about your back?" I asked.

"My back is fine," he said.

> > < <

In a little while, we had three baskets sitting on the ledge in front of the alcove. It was, I thought, an achievement. I would've been satisfied to stop there. My throat was bothering me again, and I couldn't get warm. There was a lot of wood lying around toward the front of the alcove—old roof beams, entire trunks of the same small trees that grew up on the mesa top—and I started pulling some of this wood together in the shape of a fire. The dirt was loose and messy, full of rocks and bits of charcoal and something that looked like cordage, maybe a fragment of a sandal or a yucca-fiber mat. Something to come back to.

"Do you have any matches?" I asked Prine.

"What are you doing?" Cody threw down his shovel. "You can't light a fire here," he said with the authority of a law enforcement ranger.

"I'm cold. It's this sickness coming back."

Cody said, "What if they're patrolling from the air?"

"Oh," I said. "I hadn't thought of that."

He turned away from me in disgust. Already back at work, he was digging like a terrier at the pink, ashy sand at the front of the alcove.

"Whoa whoa whoa." Prine moved fast, between me and Cody and whatever Cody had uncovered. I could see a small bundle, some cloth folded over.

"What is it?" I asked.

Cody, behind Prine, was shaking out a blanket, a ragged square of light-colored cotton with a pattern woven in.

"Let me see," I said.

Prine was blocking my way. "It's nothing. It's nothing."

"This is the shit." Cody whirled around, tossed Prine the blanket, punched me on the arm. He would never love me more.

"It's nothing," Prine said again.

But it was. It was something.

The little bundle on the ground looked at first like what it was, a tiny baby, asleep, with a peaceful look on its face; and then, after a few moments, like a mummy, wrinkling up before our eyes; and then, finally, like a shriveled leather bag.

"A blanket like that is worth a lot." Cody regarded it with respect.

"Give me that." I grabbed the blanket from Prine and laid it over the baby. I tried to be gentle but the bones shifted, with a sound like dry leaves, small and loose under the cloth.

> > < <

Prine was sitting on the edge of the low wall, cracking sunflower seeds, a ring of shells around his feet. Cody was wrapping things in newspaper and positioning them inside his pack.

"First we killed the Indians, and now we're desecrating their graves," I said, mournfully. I was still holding the baby.

"You haven't killed any Indians," Prine said. "I haven't killed any Indians." He seemed to be observing me with pity.

Cody, methodical in his packing, gestured at me to give up the blanket.

I glared at him.

"What the fuck, man?" He was astonished.

"This is the baby's blanket."

I didn't have a gun, and it occurred to me, for the first time, that Prine probably did.

Cody sighed. He came at me with open arms like an embrace. Then he was rolling up the blanket, and there was nothing but dust left on the cave floor.

Could I have done something different, and if so, what? In almost any situation that's always been my question. Everyone had said it was an accident. Even Lynne said so. But I was the one watching the baby. And later, whenever I thought about it—the couch, the cushions, the small lifeless body—the thought that went through my mind was, how could anyone be sure?

"That blanket is worth money," Prine said.

> > < <

The place we'd been working was no more than a mile and a half from the road. But on the mesa top, in the maze of gullies and the short trees, I couldn't find our two-track. I walked through the trees, toward the highway, and came out somewhere past the spot where we'd gone in. I was walking down the shoulder when the white Saab nosed out of the woods. I kept walking. Prine and Cody followed for a couple hundred yards. Then a car came up behind them and they sped up and drove away. When I couldn't see them anymore, I crossed to the other side of the highway. I put out my thumb when vehicles went by. After a while one stopped and I got in.

REVERSE ARCHAEOLOGY

I'm in Utah with Paul, who was, until last year, my boyfriend. We're in San Juan County, far enough from Moab to escape the notice of the rock climbers and the commercial mountain biking tours. We're camping under cottonwoods, off an unpaved county road.

Looking back, I can see the way we came, the narrow road through the red canyon. The air smells like rust. It's the end of March and almost hot, but there's a hint of snow blowing down from the Abajos.

On the other side of the wash is the ridge. Slabs of light-colored stone drive up out of the earth at an extravagant angle. There are canyons in the ridge, and ruins in the canyons. Four years ago, we found an artifact over there, a perfect Anasazi bowl. I've got it with me, in a box, wrapped and cushioned. It sat for eight centuries on a shelf of rock behind a juniper. Now that we're here, I'm coming down hard. It was Paul's idea to take this trip, mine to return the bowl.

Paul's busy setting up camp, threading shockcorded

poles through tent loops. He's one hundred percent focused. I can hear him breathing. It's like watching a wild animal.

"It's the right thing to do," I tell him.

"What?"

"You know."

"I know," he says. "We talked about it. We decided."

The tent jumps in the wind. We avoid each other's eyes. We're a low-impact couple in a camping ad, treading lightly. I can't imagine being here without him.

"Do you think it brought us bad luck?"

"Luck?" He shakes his head.

I persist. "We should have left it here." I'm remembering notes on the bulletin board at Petrified Forest National Park, another place we went once. *Twenty years ago I took a souvenir, it was wrong.* Regrets and consequences and rocks sent back in the mail. Why exactly did we take the bowl? At the time, it seemed like we were protecting something beautiful and rare. Like we were the ones who could keep it safe.

"Listen," Paul says.

I think he's about to confide something, but no, he's pointing out the silence. It's everywhere, a kind of membrane. It's in between the stems of this Mormon tea plant. It's in the clay underfoot, which is packed with potsherds and little chips of stone. There's a whole buried city—those gentle mounds—between the dirt road and the cliffs.

> > < <

Three days earlier: we flew in to Albuquerque, went to a wedding in Santa Fe. Paul's cousin, the bride, wore white. Forty years old and she was in her fantasy dress—satin and lace, seed pearls on the little veil. The ceremony was at the bride and groom's mesa-top adobe. A blush of snow on the mountaintops. Virginity rekindled.

In the garden, I was chatting with a woman I didn't know when Paul appeared at my side.

"How long have *you* two been married?" the woman gushed.

I didn't try to answer that one, just glanced at Paul, who said, easily, "We're not."

It wasn't the first time someone had come to that conclusion.

Later, Paul leaned against me in a half-embrace. Gave me, like a promise, the name of the place we were going next. That was his answer. I knew what was happening. We were in a John Ford western, the stagecoach going around and around what's obviously the same red rock mesa. Going west, not getting any-where.

> > < <

Under the cottonwoods, Paul and I manage the simple steps of camping with aplomb. We've done this before. We have food, and gallon jugs of water. The wolves and the grizzly bears are gone, and there's nothing to be afraid of.

I'm looking for a sign that something's changed. I know the clothes he's wearing—a familiar shirt and jeans—from other trips. He's touching me a lot. A quick kiss, a squeeze around the waist. It all feels the same.

Night falls.

"Be right back," Paul says.

I hear him open the trunk. We don't have a fire. Our lantern, a Candelier, has three tiny flames but illuminates nothing. It's something to look at.

Paul returns with a bottle—champagne, left over from the wedding—and two plastic cups.

"Toast?" he says.

I can't think of anything to drink to. "Let's just drink it."

"To adventure."

It's a boy's dream—the wild hearth, the domestic frontier. No plumbing and no house, but we know exactly how much water we have and where it's coming from.

I finish my glass quickly, and pour another. Paul's imagining, out loud, the next day's hike. He's thinking back to when we found the bowl. A different spring. Snow on the ridge, our rental sedan sashaying in the mud. We know better now, and have more money. Our rental's an SUV, something like a Conquistador or Manifest Destiny.

In the dark, he's evasive about why exactly we're on this trip together. "I thought we could see what happens."

"Hmm," I say. The champagne's going to my head. It's not that I want something to happen. It's more that I don't want *nothing*, the absence of event and consequence that, more than anything, was what spelled the end of things for us.

The bowl is on the ground between us.

"Flashlight," I request. Paul clicks it on. I can see the bowl now, out of its wrappings. The pattern inside is an all-over spiral, black-on-white, a background of fine hatched lines. Below the rim, another curve intrudes, a bit of the pattern traveling on into space. The bowl is the size of my palm across. How many times did we talk about finding something like it? There's something dumb in its perfection. Returning it has nothing to do with antiquities laws or even, really, guilt. It's more to do with the way it sits there, reminding me of the past.

"I almost threw this at you once," I say.

"I don't remember that."

"I wanted to hurt you." I say it flatly. In my head, I hear my neighbor, who's from the Philippines and an organizer par excellence. She doesn't believe in holding onto things. Pointing to some old furniture in her garage she tells me, "I can't wait to *throw it*."

"If I'd had a gun, I would have shot you." I'm pushing it with this remark. But he's not upset to hear it.

"I'm having a blast. Camping. This." He makes a gesture that takes in the cliffs, the champagne, a planet coming up bright as a city moon. His equanimity doesn't surprise me. Our relationship is a national park, preserved for rare visits.

In the tent, we arrange ourselves at a careful distance. We pull off layers of staticky fleece. The air between us fills with green sparks.

"Sorry," I say when my arm bumps his in the dark.

"It's okay."

"I'll give you some room."

He catches my hand. "No, it's okay."

"I'm not sure about this," I say. Now that the moment's here, I'm feeling uncertainty, more than desire.

"I'm not sure either."

It's all that can be said. We hold each other over the puffy bags, then push down the layers of nylon and fill. *Tread lightly*, I think. *Leave no trace*. And then we're sliding together, we've complicated things again.

> > < <

The next morning, in the canyon, I can't find the place. Not the ledge below the ruin, not the ruin. I'm stunned at my failure of memory.

Paul thinks we may have the wrong canyon. He backtracks, back to the last fork or the one before. The ridge is cut with canyon after canyon. They look a lot alike.

Heading up the slope toward an obvious alcove, I stop short. From here, I can see that this is the site. It's been looted, which is why I couldn't see it at first. The walls are down. Junk food bags and soda cans litter the ground. In the middle of it all, a woman in canvas pants and a rock art T-shirt is writing something on a clipboard.

"Please. You're on the midden." She waves me back onto the trail, and her voice trembles as she says, "I heard some people." I can't tell if she means me and Paul, or whoever's responsible for this mess.

"This place used to be untouched," I tell her.

She puts out her hand. "I'm Twyla, the site steward. This is my site."

"I didn't know rangers worked out here."

"Not a ranger, just a volunteer." She waves the clipboard like a badge. "I work with a group. We're doing a reverse archaeology project."

I don't know exactly what that means, but I'm pretty sure she'd have a heart attack if she knew what was in my pack.

"We call this the outdoor museum," she says. It's an invitation. I sense that she's lonely, and eager to talk. Forget the midden; she leads me through the site to the back of the alcove, where she points out some inscriptions, chiseled names and dates from the 1890s. "There's a written record here at this site, and other sites, that matches up with artifacts in museums, all the old collections that got shipped off back east. Back when no one kept good records. We're putting the pieces together, figuring out where things came from."

This is my site. She talks and talks. I'm going to

have to cut myself away.

When she pauses then says, "I don't see many women out hiking on their own," I seize my opportunity.

"I'm not on my own," I say. "Actually, I should be getting back. He'll think I'm lost."

Twyla blinks at me. "Your boyfriend?"

"Right."

As I head back down the canyon, then up onto the ridge, I feel things loosening. Nothing stays the same. All this preservation is overrated, in my opinion. It occurs to me that this is the first time I've been alone on this trip. From up on the ridge, I can see into Colorado, New Mexico, Arizona.

> > < <

A tumbled landscape, prickly pear on the slopes, veins of rust on the surface of the ridge. Tiny, perfect cliff dwellings look out from alcoves we can't climb up or down to. They must have used ladders, or sheer nerve, on these slopes that belly out and down with no real edge to keep you back. We're high on the ridge above our ruin.

Paul's talking about our next trip, to Alaska, or Mexico. "We're going," he says. "We're going."

I think: *We'll see what happens.*

These are far-away places. Not the difficult terrain of bedroom and kitchen, parking lot and grocery store. I'm trying not to repeat myself.

"Wait." I dig into my pack. Tell myself, *Throw it.*

The bowl is a small falling thing, nothing more. I've made more noise than this, and done more damage, hiking on talus slopes, the gravel loosening under my feet.

In the silence afterward, I clear my throat.

Paul says, "Ssh."

THE DISCOVERY OF CLIFF PALACE, MESA VERDE NATIONAL PARK

Let's destroy this park[1], you and I; let's uncap the walls, unpreserve and re-ruin it (through a process, whose early stages are said to be already underway, of budget cuts, privatization, closure, abandonment, forgetting); let's fire all the archaeologists and send the stabilization crews home[2], so that in the future it becomes possible once again to glimpse, from across the canyon, without envy[3], a lost city; to find

---

1 Established in 1906 by President Theodore Roosevelt, Mesa Verde National Park was the first national park intended to "preserve the works of man."

2 "By the 1930s, the National Park Service began ruins stabilization activities and programs that still exist today." *Implementing the Antiquities Act: A Survey of Archeological Permits 1906–1935*, by Kathleen D. Browning, National Park Service, Washington DC 2003. http://www.nps.gov/archeology/PUBS/studies/study02C.htm

3 "One must always think with envy of the entrada of Richard

one's way up cliff and down canyon, in light snow, the romantic snow of the 1880s[4]; to explore the mysterious remains of visitor centers[5], and push through oak and mountain mahogany and fendlerbush to find trash cans still holding the uncollected trash of the last days of the park; imagine there's no history; yes, let's forget even ourselves—[6]

Wetherill, the first white man who discovered the ruins in its [Mesa Verde's] canons [sic] ..." Willa Cather, "Mesa Verde Wonderland Is Easy to Reach," *Denver Times* (January 31, 1916).

4 Richard Wetherill entered Cliff Palace in December 1888. It was evidently Cather, not Wetherill, who said it was snowing. In her 1925 novel *The Professor's House* she described the moment of discovery thus: "through a veil of lightly falling snow .... a little city of stone, asleep."

5 Including Far View Visitor Center and the Chapin Mesa Archeological Museum on the mesa top, and the Mesa Verde Visitor and Research Center, opened in 2012 at the park entrance. In 1906, twenty-seven intrepid visitors toured the park. Annual visitation reached a peak of 742,080 in 1992 and has declined somewhat in the years since then.

6 And yet these footnotes remind us of the impossibility of this task; they cling to this story like the infrastructure of the very park one proposes to do away with.

THE KEEPERS

In the humidification chamber the paper takes up water vapor from the outer basin. Over the course of a few hours it relaxes visibly—the tight and brittle roll of paper loosens, it unrolls itself. With my encouragement, the edge of the map, now pliable, opens like the petal of a flower, and after a few hours I can spread it out without fear of cracking the paper and see, for the first time, what I'm looking at: a map from the last century that came to us recently from a private collection. As always with such maps, I am astonished, first at the survival of the paper, and then at the size of the lake. Our institute—the library and archives, the reading room, the exhibit gallery—is located here, where the blue of Crystal Bay ripples beneath my index finger, a spot that in those days was beneath several hundred feet of water.

I'm a conservator. My specialty is paper. I clean, deacidify, repair—but never restore, in the sense that restoration may give a misleading impression that a paper artifact is *like new*. Everything I do must be reversible. Everything is the age that it is.

I have a colleague who catalogs, one who curates exhibitions, another whose responsibility is the migration of data. We are the keepers of the lake—of the memory of the lake. We keep maps, photographs (though it's impossible to be sure of the authenticity of these images), drawings, paper records of all kinds, audiovisual materials, the whole range of items that are evidence of the former existence of this place.

In the old days, I've been told, geologists used to come quite often to do research at the institute, along with wildlife biologists, hydrologists, and others who were studying climate change. The scientists have moved on to other cataclysms. These days, though we don't like to admit it, we get mostly the antiquarians.

After the lowering of the Sierra Nevada and the transformation of the lake (more rapid than anyone anticipated) into seasonal wetlands and a vast and grassy meadow surrounding a small pond, the institute was founded to document, retroactively, the natural and cultural history of the lake. We are a not-for-profit institution, privately funded by several generous donors.

A word about provenance. This map, and the collection of which it is a part, sat for a number of years forgotten in a warehouse in Reno. This storage facility housed government records left behind by the land managing agencies when the local offices were shut down, their functions either eliminated or transferred to other agencies. Eventually those records, which by then were in a sadly deteriorated condition, were slated for the shredder or the landfill. The warehouse employees who were charged with data destruction set aside some things that seemed worth preserving. (For this we thank them.) It was from one of those workers that the collection passed to our anonymous donor.

This particular map must have been the work of an artist, I observe as I spread it between sheets of blotting paper to flatten and dry. Its beauty is excessive, beyond the needs of cartographic function. It was printed with techniques that were antique even then, on paper made of cotton, not wood pulp (in order, I realize with sudden, grateful understanding, to survive for us, the keepers). The beauty of the map has, I like to think, its own archival value; it testifies to the desire of the maker to remember.

On the map you can see the first noticeable alterations in the shoreline, the bays filling in, the silting. Here is Emerald Bay, its underwater diving park designated with an italic *CLOSED*. Here is Fannette Island, an island still.

I work in the lab all morning. In the afternoon I take a walk on one of the meadow trails that crisscross our institute grounds, where, each spring, some migratory birds persist in returning. They say that flocks of birds, who are keepers of another kind, remember ancient features of the land in their flight paths—that they swoop upwards, for instance, in order to clear the heights of volcanic peaks that have long since eroded to mere hills. Just now a golden-brown merganser came in for a landing at the edge of the meadow then flew on, with a confused flapping, to take refuge in the willow marsh, where a small body of shallow water remains, for how long we do not know.

BRISTLECONE

they'd split up before—quite a few times, in fact, though never yet successfully. This time it seemed like it might take. The man was planning to move. He'd been offered a job in another part of the country and was seriously considering it. It was, he said, an opportunity. At the last minute, while he was planning his trip to the other part of the country, to get a feel for the place and to make a decision, he asked if the woman wanted to go down there with him. They were having this conversation in the kitchen, where most of their conversations took place. The bedroom was a thing of the past. In the kitchen—his kitchen, which used to be theirs—she could hear water dripping in the sink, a small domestic erosion. In a few weeks, a month or two at the most, the kitchen would be someone else's. The woman pictured a young couple, newlyweds, one of them just out of grad school for something like architecture or graphic design. They'd have dishes. They'd have books, and bookshelves to put them on.

"Go with you, like move with you?" the woman

asked. "Or go with you on the trip."

"Go on the trip," he said.

The woman felt puny. It was like being fifteen years old again and finding out that a boy didn't like her. She played with her wine glass. She picked up the glass and scooted the coaster around the tabletop.

"Come on," he urged. "It'll be fun."

She stared at him. She considered some words then bit them back.

"We can go to some parks," he said.

Eventually she said yes to this proposal, because she wanted more than anything to say yes, even to the smallest questions.

And it was a road trip! It was fun, the first long day. They drove south from Oakland, down to Bakersfield then over Tehachapi Pass. It was dark by the time they got to Las Vegas.

Las Vegas—with the neon, and the metallic clatter of the hotel casino games, and the mirrors that made it hard to pick out the bright weary gamblers' faces from their reflections—was like being inside a television set with someone else working the remote. In the hotel bathroom, a little drunk, she got in the shower and let the water run for a long time. It felt good to be wasteful, good to be a little drunk.

The man wanted to go back down to the casino, so she went to bed by herself. She dreamed that she was hiking—a steep descent between walls of vermilion and pink. She was on this dream hike by herself. Her mouth was dry. It was so dry that soon, nothing else mattered. She tried licking her lips, tried swallowing. She had water and when she brought it to her mouth it ran off her lips and tongue, frustratingly, as if she were made of sand and rock. This happened over and over.

She woke up with a stuffy nose from the hotel air system, breathing through her mouth—the cause of the unpleasant dream. The man wasn't on his side of the bed, or in the other bed. She looked at the clock. It wasn't the middle of the night. It was only 11:30.

Zion, the next day, was a blur of sadness, a long drive through corridors of stone. Then the motel in Panguitch. A couple of white rental sedans huddled together on one side of the enormous parking lot, their back seats littered with wet towels, picnic crumbs, and badly folded maps. The woman looked inside them as she extracted her bags. Other cars, other lives. She conjured a vehicle for escape.

While the man was in the shower—was one of them always showering?—the woman went through their reading material. They were the kind of people who couldn't travel without books. She'd picked up another one at a secondhand shop in Springdale, outside Zion—the Utah volume of the old American Guide Series, put out by the Work Projects Administration. In the Zion section, the place names rang out like trumpets: Court of the Patriarchs, Temple of Sinawava. From the bathroom came the harsh fall of water, the thunk of the shampoo bottle hitting tile.

He walked out of the bathroom damp, and without a towel. After a moment, she took off her clothes. The sex wasn't bad, it had never been bad, though it was also never enough. Afterwards, she thought: If we were animals we'd stay together. She'd once read a story in a magazine, some environmental publication like *Sierra*, about a female coyote that was caught in a trap. Her mate rolled in dew so she could lick the water off his fur. The female coyote survived. A touching story the woman decided to keep to herself.

The WPA guide dated from a time when southern Utah had few paved roads, and tourists were considered men and women of courage and enterprise. In the old days, tourists had come to Panguitch for the lion hunting. They weren't satisfied with chunks of petrified wood; they wanted the skins and heads of mountain lions for souvenirs. Sitting up in bed, the woman read bits of history and natural history out loud, a stand-in for the conversation they weren't having.

In the morning they drove into the park, to an overlook, and made their way toward the rim.

The woman thought: *There is no way to do this walk with grace and beauty. Signs will be posted explaining the landmarks and the vegetation. The views will be unavoidable.*

They were tourists, and not the enterprising kind. They were part of the hubbub, the crowd handing cameras back and forth with a jovial urgency to *remember this now*.

Nevertheless, at the overlook, she looked out across the great stone amphitheater of Bryce Canyon and felt herself quiver at the spectacle, the pink extravagance. The air was full of the scent of pines.

What pines?

Forget alcohol and sex. She suspected that certain things in her life had gone wrong because of something as simple as not knowing the names of trees. A real shame, but rectifiable, right here. She applied herself to the signage. Like a student cramming for a test, convinced it wasn't too late, she skimmed the illustrated needles of ponderosa, Douglas-fir, pinyon, and bristlecone. The bristlecone pine (the text informed her) attained such astounding ages—two thousand years or more—by allowing branches to die off during periods of prolonged drought. All but one limb might die. The tree would live.

You could always count on nature for a useful metaphor. She'd make it through. Like bristlecone!

Then there was one couple left at the overlook and the man was taking their picture. He was good with cameras and with people, waiting with good humor for the other couple to settle on a pose.

"How about one of you two?" one-half of the other couple said, after the shot was taken. "Yes, we'll take one of you," said the other half of the other couple.

The man and the woman looked at each other, trapped.

Maybe refusing would have seemed to make too

big a deal of it. Maybe the other couple's enthusiasm swayed them. In those days it was film cameras, of course, the whirr of advancing film (was it a roll of twenty-four or thirty-six?) adding to the anxiety over which pictures to take. Digital was still a decade off, and with it the possibility of immediate review and deletion when an image was unflattering, out of focus, or just not something you cared to remember. When she came across that snapshot years later, she studied it as she had once studied the guidebook and trail signage. It was an artifact now, startling in its instructiveness. A man she used to know; the woman she used to be; at the edge of the frame, unforgettable, the pale and limber twists of a bristlecone pine.

THE CURATION OF SILENCE

1 Notes on Silence
The curation of silence is nearly a lost art. Professional curators consider it old-fashioned. In the seventeenth century, cabinets of curiosities frequently included specimens of silence housed in porcelain jars. Scientist-explorers undertook voyages of discovery and brought back new undreamed-of silences carefully packed in excelsior and cotton. Containers are essential for the safekeeping of silences, though very small silences may be pinned to a velvet-covered board. You may keep one indefinitely, preserved in ethyl alcohol, in a tightly sealed jar. A silence pickled in this way has a strong odor of the past. To the novice, a silence may appear identical with the form of its container. Once in a while, one stumbles on silences in neglected corners of out-of-the-way museums, in an old vitrine, perhaps, or on a dusty shelf of specimen jars with cork or glass stoppers, brimful of some stained liquid. They resemble the claustrophobic natural history collections in which formerly living flesh,

pale, coiled, and fetal in appearance, is preserved in jars like glass wombs whose size is a frank acknowledgment that the contents need no room for respiration and movement. Sometimes you find such jars mysteriously drained, with traces of granular residue clinging to the sides. Even in this deteriorated state, such containers eloquently lay claim to their true contents, which some say is memory, others say is time itself.

Casanova admired the labels, inlaid in ivory, on the mahogany shelves of a Venetian doge's library, records of a collection that was already lost: *silentium africanum, silentium maritimum*. In Britain in the eighteenth century, follies were constructed by collectors who had the resources to support the earnest contemplation of their silences. Learned societies of amateur amphorologists, sometimes called vesselists, met to drink, smoke, and exchange specimens. A silence does not exist without its collector. American antiquarians specialized in colonial silences, some retrieved from Britain after the Revolutionary War. Jeremy Belknap, founder of the Massachusetts Historical Society, had a penchant for entering unattended private homes to rescue historical records from what he called the "garrets and ratholes of old houses" ("There is nothing like having a *good repository* and keeping a *good look out*, not waiting at home for things to fall into the lap, but prowling about like a wolf for the prey," he wrote) and is credited thereby with the accidental preservation of numerous early American silences. At the manor house in Söderfors in Sweden, a famous *naturaliekabinett*—Linnaeus studied it—superseded a cabinet of silences from diverse geographic locales obtained through representatives of the Swedish East India Company and brought back in lacquer boxes and jars of Chinese porcelain. It may be that the lord of the manor, Adolf Ulric Grill, found silences a restful contrast to the ever-present clanging of the massive water hammers at the Söderfors anchor works. Grill's six hundred stuffed birds went to the Royal Swedish Academy of Sciences. The fate of his silence collection is unknown.

The collecting of silences may be compared to the sampling of ice cores to determine the taste of the water drunk by woolly mammoths, or the snatching of air from a sealed Egyptian tomb or an insect's amber chamber to analyze ancient atmospheres. Yet historians of science, when they consider silence collections at all, dismiss them as a historical footnote. As a branch of museology, it has largely been subsumed into the study of containers. In the 1920s, silences were associated with Egyptology and the occult, Conan Doyle and fairy photographs. As for the curation of silence, it is what museums aspire to but they content themselves with artifacts, Lord Carnarvon is said to have remarked. Connoisseurs know that no two silences are alike. They have no intrinsic value. But a copy of the *Encyclopédie de silences divers et universelles* printed in Paris in the year 1752 sold at auction last year at Sotheby's books and manuscripts for a very respectable price.

In addition to silences both natural and artificial, the history of the curation of silence may also encompass:

> Mythical silences—the unicorns and gryphons of museology.

> False silences, fakes; unprovenienced silences.

> Books, including manuscript or printed

catalogues of collections that are no longer extant. Some antique silences are known only from their descriptions. Extra-illustrated books are a nineteenth-century curiosity; librarians dislike them because their pages, thick with inserted silences, cannot easily be closed.

> Silences do not exist in reproduction form.

Now, silences have fallen out of fashion. In the future, we may invent other means to consider and commemorate our vanishments. One day our museums may lose their function, and their architecture may puzzle our descendants. One day we may return to the ideal once represented by the cabinet and the jar.

2. Sherds

When I copied the foregoing notes on silence, I was an intern at the new regional archaeological repository in southwest Colorado, a facility developed to handle the shortage of space (aka the curation crisis) in the museums in the Four Corners states. I reported to the collections manager, a woman in her late thirties named Nanette Fields. On my first day, she started me on ceramics. "We've got a backlog," she said cheerfully, as if a backlog were a good thing.

"OK!" I mirrored her level of enthusiasm precisely. I wasn't sure I wanted a museum career, but I was trying it out and wanted to do my best.

The repository anchored one end of the Montezuma County Mall, a sprawling, sand-colored structure fighting for its dignity in the face of abandonment. The JC Penney closed last year. The college had taken over some of the storefronts for classroom space—beauty in the old salon, culinary arts in the family-style restaurant. Everyone believed that learning new skills was an important and valuable thing. A few stores hung on in the vicinity of the food court, with its potted palm trees and its fountain surrounded by pebbled concrete. We got a discount at the coffee place. Outside the mall there was a view of Mesa Verde and Sleeping Ute, pretty much standard for the 5MT—which was the prefix for archaeological site numbers in the county.

As for me, I worked in a windowless room, inventorying and rehousing collections. Mainly, I counted sherds: pieces of broken pottery from the Ancestral Puebloan culture. The artifacts I was working with had been collected in the 1970s; the sherds were in 1970s plastic bags fastened with 1970s twist ties, and housed in 1970s cardboard boxes. I got to know the weight of overstuffed boxes, the feel of the fibrous yellow tape you could flick off with a finger and the disintegrating paper labels. The bags were deteriorating; some were flimsy sandwich bags that had grown sticky with age. When I opened a box I could smell the off-gassing from the plastic, and sometimes the bags split when I picked them up, spilling sherds onto the tray—we used old school cafeteria trays to sort and count. This was necessary work: the preservation of the artifacts, rehousing them into new archival-quality bags and boxes, and the database updates that would let researchers access the collections. It was also dusty and tedious. Most of my sherds were gray ware, as ordinary as a sherd could be. There were other kinds of ceramics, red ware and white ware, but for some reason I got mostly gray, and not even the named types like Moccasin Gray, Mancos Gray, Lino Gray, or Mummy Lake Gray. They were just gray. Some of the sherds were black and sooted, and those I liked. I could feel how much they'd been used; I could almost smell the pot of beans stewing on the hearth, an intuition so vivid it seemed like something I'd experienced myself. But for the most part, counting gray ware was like counting sheep. Sherd crumbs, which were basically dirt, would get under my fingernails. I'd wash and dry my hands so many times in a day that my knuckles would crack and bleed. But when Nanette brought a back-room tour through, I said I loved the work. It could have been worse. I could have been working on coprolites or bulk indeterminate ground stone.

By the end of the first week I'd gotten the hang of it, and by week two the work was routine. If anyone could have seen how I spent my days, it would have looked as if I were playing a weird, boring game: solitaire with sherds and bags and labels. There was an occasional diversion, like a note from the original lab staff or field crew. On the field bag, next to the collection date, it would say something like "first day of summer" or "my birthday." Once I found a note to the curators of the future, asking us please to call if this box was ever opened again. I dialed the number. I reached a widow, who was interested but forgetful. "My first husband was an archaeologist. What was his name? I was married to him for sixteen years."

Nanette would joke with me about the sherds. "There are more where those came from! It's job security!"

She was right. There were more sherds—long rows of boxes full of them in the repository. Some of them, I imagined, must have come from the land that the mall was built on. Sometimes I'd think, *did they really need to collect all of them?* I was always longing for a break and some sunlight, a quick walk around the parking lot. Sometimes I'd go past the edge of the lot into the field. There was a site out there in the sagebrush, with sherds on the ground, which were more interesting than sherds in bags. Most people didn't know about that site. At other times when I got bored, I would slip into the library, a little room outside the locked repository doors. There was a comfortable chair that couldn't be seen by anyone walking by in the hallway, and I could spend an hour unobserved with books that I picked out at random from the shelves. That was how I learned about the curation of silence. It was the subject of Nanette's thesis, a slender volume bound in red buckram that opened stiffly to reveal clean, unread pages. In none of her workplace behavior did she ever give any sign of the eager scholar she had been a decade earlier. Indeed, whenever I asked her a question she seemed mildly surprised, as if curiosity were not in my job description.

3. Curiosities

One day, Nanette called me into her office. She seemed harried, and when she told me about the special project that was coming up, I understood why. We would be part of the team sent to pack the artifacts being confiscated in the Odegard case.

"Wear something tan," she told me. That was so I would blend in with the regular staff—a way of looking unofficially official. She looked askance at what I happened to have on that day: a party dress I'd pulled, wrinkled but unstained, from the Telluride Free Box. She meant pants and a shirt.

The Odegard property lay northwest of Blanding, Utah. It was an out-of-the-way part of the world, north of the Navajo Reservation and in the center of a vast area of canyon and mountain country more populous in Ancestral Puebloan times than today. The Odegards were not native Utahns—they came to the Four Corners from Brooklyn, New York, in the 1970s—but Mr. Odegard had taken to the local custom of pothunting. He was charged with a number of violations of the Archaeological Resources Protection Act, the first high-profile case since the cases of 2009 that brought so much unwanted publicity to this area. Most unusually for this kind of case, Mrs. Odegard had turned her husband in herself.

"You're late," she said when we arrived.

I liked her immediately. She reminded me of my grandmother, with her housecoat and Brooklyn accent. Her apron pocket showed the unmistakable outline of a cigarette pack.

Mr. Odegard's collection filled the modest ranch house, which resembled a museum of the local history variety in its cluttered approach to display. Framed on the wall of the foyer, the name *Odegard* was spelled out in tiny arrowheads. Artifacts were in every room, even the kitchen and the bathroom and in the hallway. Mrs. Odegard, we realized, could not wait to clean house. She'd emptied the closets and piled the dining room table high with Indian baskets and spear points. There were ceramics, both modern and prehistoric, from an old trading post, with pawn tags attached, and most notoriously, as had been widely reported, items from a dry cave in the Nevada desert dating to approximately nine thousand years ago. Mrs. Odegard flung open the doors of the china cabinet. All of the serving pieces were stacked on one side; Indian baskets took up the rest of the space. The smell of the baskets filled the dining room with the odor of honey and hay. I caught one basket—Paiute, I guessed—before it toppled out. It felt heavy, as if there were something in it. The weight came from the density of the weave. The stitches were close, fine, and even, making a flexible basketwork that looked and felt like thick cloth. In the design, a dark butterfly rose above a row of mountain peaks on a honey-colored background. I brought it to my nose and breathed in the strong, sweet smell of the fibers.

"Do me a favor and get rid of this trash," Mrs. Odegard said. She heaved a sagging cardboard box onto the floor, where it split open, spilling sherds everywhere.

Nanette sighed. She was supervising a crew of five, and my presence seemed to be superfluous. She gave me the assignment of keeping Mrs. Odegard out of the way, so she could do her assessment without interference. She looked hard at me. "Are you crying?" she asked.

She assumed that I was moved by the sight of all those artifacts, illegally obtained and in private hands, a good many of them probably from burial contexts. The truth was my boyfriend had dumped me *that very morning* and my heart was heavy with memories. My pockets were full of them.

I led Mrs. Odegard out onto the back porch, where I bummed a cigarette. (You'd be surprised how many curators and archaeologists smoke.)

"Did she kick you out, too?" Mrs. Odegard asked.

I nodded. "Odegard," I said. "That's Norwegian, isn't it?"

"Abandoned farm. It's a name from the Black Death days." She stubbed out her cigarette. "Come on, dear. I'll show you my silence collection."

Behind the house were a number of dilapidated outbuildings including a little trailer, old, weather-beaten, with tires on the roof and a good view to the west. The trailer, I discovered, was a most unusual cabinet of curiosities. Mrs. Odegard's collection was household and domestic in form, yet the silences spanned the range of human habitation in the New World, from PaleoIndian through the late twentieth century. She kept them in household containers. Apothecary, Mason, and Ball jars were her ampho-rae. Also, desiccated snow domes of cheap plastic, Mormon buckets with airtight lids, Tupperware and paint cans, shoeboxes (ladies' size seven), an old-fashioned hatbox, a child's lunch box—to name just a few. No container was too humble to hold its por-tion of the past. In this assemblage, I was excited to recognize a form of folk curation, vernacular and very American. I also understood why she wanted to get rid of her husband's artifacts. For years, her own collection had been relegated to the sheds and the trailer, where they baked in the summer and froze in the winter. She wanted space in the house.

As she described her items, I felt the implications of the Odegard name, so evocative of the high mountain valleys of Norway, depopulated by plague, and the abandoned farms claimed by those who had survived and who would carry the memory of that abandonment in the names they took.

Although she was a collector, and a passionate one, Mrs. Odegard was adamant that the silences were not to go to a museum after her death. She disliked museums. She believed that they imposed an unnatural concern with preservation upon a material world whose natural end was to decay.

I promised I wouldn't say a word to my boss—who looked in the trailer while we were there, and saw nothing of interest. I didn't tell her, I suppose, because she was not in the habit of soliciting my opinion. If she knew the nature of Mrs. Odegard's collection she would certainly have found some pretext for accessioning it.

I assured Mrs. Odegard the government had no interest in her silence collection. ARPA did not cover the taking of silences from public or Indian lands.

Later, when I told this story, people have

responded: *What a ridiculous and pointless enterprise!*
And some have asked me if she was a hoarder. To
which I would answer: *Everything is a container. The
box, the jar, the house, the museum, the body.*

4. Visible Curation

After my internship, I graduated to paid employ-
ment at the same facility, working in visible curation.
It was a new venture, a public-private curation con-
cession. The idea was to show the public what went
on behind the scenes. Mostly, I counted sherds. At
ten in the morning, facilities rolled up the gate and
voila. There I was, in a lab coat, working behind a plate
glass window. It attracted quite a bit of interest, as an
example of public outreach and adaptive reuse of the
mall. People took photos sometimes. Why was this
interesting? No one would stand outside a window
watching a librarian check out books.

I didn't get the job because of my looks but my
looks didn't hurt. Donations in the box and gift shop
sales went up during my shift. The down side was
that every once in a while I'd have to call security
and report that someone was watching me in a way I
didn't feel comfortable with. During my orientation,
I'd seen film footage of the Glen Canyon archaeological project in Utah. Men—boys, really, shirtless and
tan, in shorts—did the fieldwork; girls worked in the
lab. The collections were sent up to Salt Lake City. In
the film, the door of the lab opens, and we see the lab

girl—it's something like 1960—in a shirtwaist dress, ready to wash the dishes and put them away. It was a little erotic, being watched while I worked. I wasn't supposed to interact, or even make eye contact. Sometimes I'd pick the most boring tasks on purpose. People who thought museums kept the best stuff in storage—well, I'd show them. No crystal skulls here! I'd wash artifacts. I'd spend an hour scrubbing sherds with an old toothbrush.

This morning, Nanette wheeled out from the repository the largest box of sherds I'd ever seen. It filled almost the whole length and width of one of our gray plastic carts, the Luxor model with the silhouette of Nefertiti on the handle. Inside the box was an enormous bag, of a heavyweight plastic that felt greasy to the touch, and—*yow*—a straight pin stuck through the knot that kept the bag shut. The bag was full of gray ware body sherds. A piece of cake. The sherds all had the same field specimen and catalog number. This meant an easy database update: one catalog record, rather than hundreds of individual records for hundreds of individual sherds.

After a half-hour or so, I got the unpleasant feeling that I'd lost count. Something had distracted me—some visitor activity on the other side of the glass, Nanette waltzing through saying "Job security!" or just my own thoughts. Often, while counting sherds, my thoughts would wander back to the day I'd spent in Blanding. Sometimes, surrounded by rehoused

collections—a blank wall of beige and gray and brown
archives and curation boxes, a peculiarly disheartening
landscape—I would feel an almost irresistible urge to
de-house the collections, return them to their nature
as individual artifacts, and if they were perishable, let
them decay.

In any case, I lost count and became convinced
that I'd been counting the same sherds over and over.
They all looked more or less the same, and yet, I had
one in my hand, with some distinctive incising on it,
that I had definitely counted before.

There was nothing to do but sweep the avalanche
of sherds off the tray into the box and start over.

It was a big box of gray ware sherds, let me tell
you.

Each sherd was individually nondescript. En
masse, they started to seem malevolent, like birds in
a Hitchcock film.

It occurred to me that the repetitive nature of this
work was exactly what an observer might find erotic:
the way I did the same thing over and over, when it
couldn't possibly give me any pleasure. In visible curation, first and foremost was touch, the handling and
caretaking of objects. In some sense, all of this work
was erotic; it was about what we were doing in the
present, not about preserving the past.

I'd been dating someone new for a few weeks. We
met for lunch at the food court. Sparrows were hopping around up in the rafters. We couldn't see them,

but we could hear them twittering—they'd moved in with the cold weather.

"How's work today?" he asked.

"It's all right," I said. "I'm doing ceramics inventory."

He yawned and started leafing through a copy of the newspaper that was discarded at the next table. He had no interest in my work, which was a quality I found very attractive in a man.

"People pay to watch me work. Do you think that's kind of, well, erotic?" I asked.

"Counting sherds?" He snorted. "No."

When I got back from lunch, the contents of the box seemed to have actually expanded in my absence, like a plate of spaghetti at a family restaurant. That could happen. Sometimes, when you opened a box where everything had sort of settled over the years, the sherds would expand into available space.

"How's it going with that box?" Nanette asked.

"It's going," I said. "It's job security!"

I'd counted well over two thousand sherds, yet the box seemed as full as ever. There was definitely something strange about it. No wonder there was a backlog.

And yes, I could have been counting faster, but—well, you try it sometime.

What exactly were they longing for, those people on the other side of the glass? Maybe a past that wasn't ours, a romanticized past of cliff dwellers and ruins, a time that existed apart from us, Indians that we didn't kill.

At the big museums back east, like the Smithsonian and the Metropolitan Museum of Art, I loved to enter the European rooms: whole rooms that had been extracted from palaces, shipped to America, and reconstructed. I wondered if ghosts ever traveled with those collected rooms, and if they were wandering confused in American cities, or if they embraced immigration in the afterlife. Just as nature is more than the artificial consolations to be found within the boundaries of a park, the museum of the past is everywhere. Today at lunch, when I read in the newspaper of the death of Mrs. Odegard, I knew that her silence collection had passed away with her. To collect was not only to preserve, but also to alter through the addition of new meanings—just as the books on my shelf were becoming an autobiography of myself that would also be dispersed someday—meanings which were individual, personal, and destined to fade away without a trace.

GOING TO RANDSBURG

at the post office, at the drug store, at Smith's, sometime in April, people started asking each other, *Are you going to Randsburg?* To Sarah, who was still new in town, the question became one of those expressions that comes to stand for a generic greeting. The way, in another language, asking *Have you eaten?* means *How are you?*

Randsburg was the privately owned hot springs in the forest outside of town. Traditionally, it opened around Memorial Day weekend, depending on road conditions. (Neither that stretch of the state road nor the forest road was plowed.)

Sarah had asked someone what was so special about Randsburg. Weren't there other hot springs in Idaho? "There's lithium in the water," she was told. Aside from this one fact, Randsburg remained legendary and undescribed—a name in the forest. Thinking that the local hot springs would be a photographed attraction, Sarah had looked for it in the drugstore's postcard racks, without success.

"I'm thinking about it," she answered, when people

asked her if she was going. That was always the answer one gave. It implied that Randsburg was only the nearest option and that life offered many other choices.

> > < <

Their house was in the woods, near the river. Standing at the kitchen window, washing dishes slowly, sometimes Sarah would see a fox.

By the first day of spring, one hundred thirty-five inches of snow had fallen. All through April and into the first week of May, it snowed. The old snow slumped under the eaves, taking on human shape in the shadows of early evening as Sarah walked the dogs. She had the road to herself. She still wasn't used to so much emptiness. No city. No men in doorways, under cardboard. Most of the houses on their road were still closed up for the winter. They had sensible owners who had other homes in California or Arizona or even Boise. Sarah corrected herself: especially Boise. Someone from Boise would know what the winters were like up here. She imagined all that snow piled up at once: twelve feet of it.

The river ran in a wide swath at the bottom of the road. The river was different these days, widening and rising. Big trees stood at intervals along its banks, a giant's palisade. The dead trees were called snags— Sarah recited the nature lesson, from the bird book or the tree book—and snags were habitat for birds. She looked up, and there was the messy brown bowl of an osprey's nest.

Kirk's dogs—she still thought of them as Kirk's dogs—snuffled along the riverbank; they slurped the icy water. Everything was interesting, everything had its smell. Sarah called them. "Aldo! Pumpkin!" They heard the lack of conviction in her voice and raised their heads quizzically. "Come join us!" they woofed. "Come and play!" The late afternoon sun had reglazed the rutted snow and mud. She slipped, almost fell. "Aldo!" she called, meaning it now. "Pumpkin!"

At home it was cleanup time. No mud was allowed in the house in the woods. The dogs had their own towels, new and plush.

"OK," she said, opening the door to the hallway. "Go."

Then, finally, it was her turn. She poured a glass of wine. Good girl. A biscuit for Sarah. But what had she done to deserve a reward? This was the simplified life, the one that other women envied her for. She could bake, she could do something with all of that yarn. The women in the knitting magazines led gorgeous lives, with skeins of yarn on the porch. Nothing gathered dust. You saw their husbands at a distance, chopping wood, wearing interesting sweaters. (They were always husbands, never boyfriends.) The orchard was in bloom. Apple blossoms drifted.

Yesterday's yoga tape was still in the VCR. She got comfortable on the couch, drowsing over a magazine, and then Kirk called.

"Hi," she said, startled to find it was dark. She

must have fallen asleep.

"How was your day?"

The dogs pranced underfoot, hearing Kirk.

"Great," she said. "I saw an osprey nest. Down by the river. It was huge."

Kirk was in California, working. That was the whole idea: to have the perfect house, someplace in the country, but with an airport in town, so Kirk could get in and out.

"Are you OK with this?" he was asking.

She stared out into the dark room. What had he just told her? Something about the project, another meeting. He would be gone a few more days. That was the thing with cell phones: they clipped the ends off words, and you were constantly thinking that you might have missed something important. She hadn't, though.

"I'm OK with it," she said. "I've got lots to do here."

> > < <

When they first announced their plans to move to Idaho, both her family and Kirk's had reacted as if they had said "Antarctica." Someone gave them, as an unironic gift, a copy of *Where There Is No Doctor*. They had fun, at first, defying their families and declaring their sense of adventure. Then Kirk followed through on his plans for consulting work. He was gone for a week or two—sometimes longer. He went places where the sun was warm and there were expensive hotels with swimming pools and bars. Sarah could hear the pool-splash and clink of glassware behind his hasty cell phone check-ins.

And then most mornings she would wake up to the thick felt of new snow. Kirk would be back in California, and Sarah had to clear the porch steps, in heavy boots and yesterday's jeans. It was becoming a problem, one she would bring up if Kirk ever came back for long enough to have a serious talk.

Sarah had another problem too, but not one she was going to discuss with Kirk.

The problem was Jackson, who was housesitting in the big log house at the top of the road. She walked the dogs up there, sometimes. Not too often. He was in graduate school for wildlife biology, and on some kind of leave—lucky for his cousins, who would otherwise have had to pay one of the housekeeping services in town. Sarah's heart took a small, giddy leap whenever Jackson drove by in his truck. When she enumerated the bounty of her life—a husband, a Jeep, a house with rooms, a room for everything—Jackson was a part of it.

Winter, spring, the return of the cousins. Sarah had spent too much time thinking about this—the waters that would sweep this man away from her.

This morning, the first of May, the railings and the shrubs were dripping. It was ten o'clock in the morning and it was above freezing, barely.

Sarah looked at her watch again, as if she had an appointment to keep.

"Stay," she said to the dogs, who were at the door, then the window, misting the glass with their eager breath.

She saw him just as she made the sloppy turn into the Smith's parking lot, lurching through slush. He was outside the store, as if he'd been waiting for her. He was looking reliable in jeans, work boots, an orange coat with the oily-looking surface that old down jackets get. She had seen him move snow in that coat. Once, she'd woken up to the sound of something shattering—Jackson, knocking ice off the eaves of her house.

He took a step forward, triggering the door-opening mechanism.

"Hey," he said.

"Hey," she said, gliding through.

The grocery store was a dream of spring, crowded up front with a display of patio tables, folding chairs, bottles of OFF! and citronella candles. With an effort of will, Sarah ignored these products. She held off spring, summer, the world in which she and Jackson would never have sex.

"Want some coffee?" Jackson said.

She followed him to the store's espresso corner—three tiny tables with an urban sleekness, next to the milk and the cheese. They had a conversation. (Subjects: dogs, the persistence of snow.) Her real thoughts took form and melted away like snow crystals. Not something she'd marshal into a sentence. Not something she'd ever say.

"Kirk's out of town," she offered.

"The winters here will get to you," Jackson said. He was still talking about the snow!

He leaned back. "I was thinking about going to Randsburg today."

"But they're closed," she said. "Aren't they?"

This was the big news in town, the great disappointment. Something had happened—a death or an ownership crisis of some kind. There was no definite explanation, but everyone had heard that Randsburg wasn't opening this year.

"Well," he said. "The *store* might be closed. No one's *working* there." He looked an invitation at her.

She could sit there drinking her little coffee. She could go back home and dissect her own loneliness.

"What's so great about Randsburg, anyway?" she asked, flirting.

"There's lithium in the water." Jackson grinned.

> > < <

Randsburg was twenty miles out of town, on a highway that ran straight through monotonous second-growth forest. Sarah felt small and untethered, daringly without a seatbelt, in the cab of Jackson's truck. Trapped by winter, she'd hardly left town since Christmas. It was two hours to Boise in good weather, the one thing you couldn't count on that year.

She stole a glance at Jackson. He was driving intently, watching the road. She was relieved at his silence; he didn't seem to expect anything of her.

This is how it happens, she thought. Things fall into place. She wasn't thinking of a new start, nothing like that—all she wanted was to step into the middle of something. Later, she'd step back out. The world was full of such opportunities. As Kirk well knew.

There was a gate across the road, a loop of wire around a post. She jumped down to open it. The truck rolled through. The road was a white bed of snow where the trees weren't. The woods were dark.

(Survival plans. Sarah took inventory: she had boots, a good coat. No matches, though. Jackson wasn't in this dream. This one was hers alone: Sarah lost in the woods, a little girl following a trail of crumbs.)

"Hey, look," she said when she got back in the truck and they were moving again. "Elk."

The herd was in a meadow on the other side of a thin line of trees, stock still, with heads lifted, alert, acknowledging the vehicle.

Sarah said, "They're in Idaho and they don't know it."

Jackson nodded a reply. Probably just being polite. Lately, Sarah had spent so much time alone, she could not distinguish between things that were worth saying and things best kept to herself.

Never mind. She knew what she meant. It had come over her often since moving up here—this awareness of where she was, in a place that was new and strange. These moments skinned off the hide of routine that always threatened to grow over her life, even here. *I am in a grocery store in Idaho*, she would think. *I am putting gas in my car in Idaho.*

Randsburg came into view. A low wooden fence, a gate—this one with a lock—and steam rising from the other side. Sarah followed Jackson, stepping up onto a stump and over the fence.

So this was Randsburg, this was what all the fuss was about. A cluster of brown wooden shacks at the bottom of a little valley. A dozen or so falling-down cabins stood on the slopes opposite, in a forest of stumps. Downslope stood a row of privies. She could see all the way to the other side of the river, another meadow, another herd of elk. The pool was huge, and lined with logs, a drowned cabin. She could feel the warm air hanging over the water.

Jackson pushed open the door of a weathered building—nothing was locked on the other side of the fence. There was candy behind glass, on dusty shelves. Even the dirt looked old. Sarah couldn't see the roof beams, and only dimly, the sides of the room. Next to an antique cash register, a stack of last year's brochures, water-stained, advertised Cabins for Rent. The building smelled of stale air and wet wood.

Jackson took her hand. His fingers curled past hers to write a message of desire in her palm. This was sweeter than she expected, and more alarming.

"Things can get pretty primitive up here," Sarah said in a voice that was not hers but her husband's, making them out to be some sort of pioneers to the folks back home.

"Here we go," Jackson said, opening a cabinet. "Towels but no bathing suits."

Sarah took her towel and went outside, to the other side of the pool where a sign on an outbuilding said Ladies Changing Room. It was pitch dark inside. She pushed the door back, finding the rock that served as doorstop on the hard dirt floor, and undressed in the gray, cloudy light. Her skin goosepimpled in the cold.

She was going to seduce a man in Idaho.

She froze, looking toward the half-open door. Had she said it out loud? *Get a grip, Sarah.*

Jackson was already in the water, looking serene, when she came out. She shivered as she dropped her towel, feeling all legs and shoulders, her skinny ninth-grade self.

"You left your underwear on," he said.

"Are you disappointed?" This was not her voice either. This was someone from a movie, some actress.

"No," he said. "No."

"Close your eyes." She hurried out of the ridiculous lace and went down the log steps, which were green with algae and slick underfoot. At the bottom her feet touched sand. "Hot," she said, involuntarily. "OK, you can open your eyes now."

The pool was all one depth and deeper than she expected—the water came up to her collarbones.

Through the steam, everything was gray and wavering. The cabins and trees looked blurry, like a newspaper photograph up close. This was the cooler end; at the top was another tiny pool, the source of the springs.

Jackson went under, suddenly. Sarah stepped back, keeping her head up, afraid he would grab her underwater. But he came up in the same place, his hands full of the dark sand that was at the bottom of the pool. He sluiced water over his hands and examined them.

"What are you doing?" she asked.

He tipped his hands to show her. There were bits of something tiny, dark red and sparkling in the sand. Garnets. She touched one of the tiny crystals off his palm.

"I want to find some," she said and dropped under water. She came up dripping, the sand running out of her hands.

They wavered, almost touching.

Then Sarah said something idiotic and embarrassing and intended to fend him off. There was an attraction. Undeniably. But already, she felt, it might as well be over. Just going to Randsburg—wasn't that enough? She didn't have to do anything else. She could just keep soaking in the hot, lithium-rich water until she stopped wanting inappropriate things.

> > < <

The cabins were up the slope, in front of the trees. They looked like they were from the nineteenth century, like miners' cabins with sagging roofs and wide cracks between the boards. They remembered what sickness was, and lust for metal, and killing Indians.

The room was long and narrow. There was a bed with a quilt on it. A wood stove. The wind was rattling the door in the frame and sifting in around the small window.

He touched first, catching her with his fingers between her legs. They kissed with cold, open mouths. She felt chilled and slow—the shock of contact with his body a collision she needed to recover from.

The store had yielded condoms, from behind the counter, and extra blankets.

"I think I need some time," she said.

> > < <

And then they are in bed, with the sheet pulled up, and the blankets smelling of mothballs piled on top.

"I've never felt cotton like this," Sarah is saying. She's talking because she's nervous. The sheets are something from another era, much laundered and bleached to a luminous snow-white. The cotton *is* different—thick and soft and heavy.

She turns her head and catches him looking at her. "What?" she demands. Prickly, like a teenager.

She can't think of anything that he might want to hear.

It doesn't matter. Jackson seems to be floating over her, and she sees the contours of his face in close-up, magnified and a little distorted. Kirk had looked strange like that, too, their first few times. It makes her think of ultrasounds she's seen, all eyes and nose, weird, though recognizably human. It makes her think of the elk in their elk world.

He pushes inside her in a husbandly way, as if he has known her for a long time, and as if this all makes sense to him.

This is what she wanted.

> > < <

Back in his truck, on their way back to town, she pulled down the visor to check her face, but there wasn't any mirror.

"I must look awful," she said.

He gave her a searching look.

The air, which had been so damp and gray and still all day, began to stir. A few tentative flakes, then a squall of snow pellets that rattled the vehicle on all sides. Then, for some long minutes, a blizzard, riotous and obscuring the way ahead.

"It's snowing?" Sarah stared out at the curtains of white. She'd be home in half an hour if they didn't slide off the road.

"It's just flurries," Jackson said.

He pressed his foot on the gas, as if spring were only a little farther down the road and he could take her there.

She wondered frantically how to get rid of him.

UTAH WILDMALL RANGERS

When the help desk call comes in—it's rock-fall this time, on the Rim Trail—I head out in my Jeep. Another day at Utah Canyons.

> > < <

Spacious skies and purple mountains, majesty and grace and an award-winning Image Management Plan. Our scenic values are off the charts. From daybreak through sunset and on into the night with our dark sky program, it's all in the IMP.

> > < <

Sometimes on my rounds I used to drive down one of the Seldom Seen roads that wanders off across the flats to the northwest, old mining or cattle-driving roads with a feeling of the Old West, desolate and parched and hopeless. All of these roads dead-end in the same area, a box canyon whose entrance is concealed behind a cottonwood that's half fallen over. There's nothing scenic about it. It's basically Not Seen. On the other side of the park boundary, I'd sit on a flat rock and look at nothing in particular. Scuff my boots in some dust, throw a pebble over the edge.

> > < <

Utah Canyons is America's first wildmall. Tourists come by the busload. Our motto is NATURE. OWN IT. It's an interagency partnership between Utah Parks and the BLM. We've got advantages over traditional parks. You can't take a bad picture here. It's a question of angles and sight lines, temperature and relative humidity. The weather is predictable. Rainbows appear at 4 and 6 on summer afternoons. The scenic dustings of snow run November through March. Our park manager has an MBA and an undergrad degree in Desert Adventure.

> > < <

I take my time. I park at the rim lot, kill a few minutes watching two girls striking sassy poses with nature's splendor arrayed behind them. Sunset shadows are creeping along the east face, lengthening with perceptible jolts. It's a little alarming—the speed of it like time-lapse footage, plus it's only two in the afternoon—but the girls don't seem to notice.

Things have been off lately. The discomfort index has been way up, and some visitors have asked for their money back. IT's out here on a regular basis.

Not my problem, not since the day my supervisor called me into his office. My supervisor looked like Humphrey Bogart, right down to the khaki uniform trousers that he wore belted high, and he sounded like him, too. It's high tech out here, but lonesome. We watch a lot of Netflix. Walk past the housing units at night and you see the flicker of screens in the windows, the blue campfires that keep us warm.

He cued up the security footage, fast-forwarding through segments until he got to a sequence: some old roads, a nondescript little canyon, a blurry figure exiting a blurry state vehicle.

"Let's talk about this footage and let's talk about it straight." He jabbed a finger at the paused screen. "That looks like you, kid."

As a viewshed analyst, this surprised me. Line of sight, corridor management—how could I have screwed this up? He ran it by me again, frame by frame. I squinted at the monitor.

"It might be me," I admitted, "but I can't be sure."

"As a supervisor, when you see something like this, you're supposed to do something about it."

In this way, I was demoted from image management specialist to seasonal ranger. Right back where I started from.

The job's not bad, though. In some ways I've got it better than before. I work eight tens, then I'm off six—which beats five days a week of nine-to-five. I patrol the frontcountry, the souvenir trails. When you register at the trailhead, you're authorizing credit card charges for the pictures that you take and any rocks and fossils that end up in your pocket. As a way of life, it's as good as any. I make a living in a place where, most of the time, I want to be. I remind myself that the simulated protects the real.

Down in the canyon, about a hundred feet below the rim, I run into Landry, from the entrance station. It must be his day off; he's out of uniform, in shorts and a ratty T-shirt from Ray's Tavern in Green River. He seems to be pushing a real boulder up the trail. He looks at my boots, then up at me, then back at the rock under his hands.

"Ah, crap," he says.

My work's routine. When I started here ten years ago I used to do trail maintenance, but now that all the trails have been upgraded to self-maintaining it's really pretty boring. So whatever Landry's up to off-duty, I'm probably going to be OK with it. Of course, he doesn't know that.

"Is there a problem here?" I ask, one Utah WildMall Ranger to another. I don't know him that well. Landry's just a few years out of school, still gung-ho and baby-faced, though his pack is enormous and ratty. We've had a few beers in Moab. We've bullshit-ted a little.

"I got a call about some rockfall. Know anything about it?" I'm channeling Bogey. To my surprise, interrogation works. Landry says he thinks he may have tripped a sensor somewhere.

"Goddammit," I say.

Pretty soon he's singing like a canary. He says he's had it with touchable pixels. He confesses that he's been packing in unauthorized material. He smuggles in gnats, in vials. He sifts red dust into vehicles as they pass through the entrance station. When it comes to tripping hazards the man is a genius.

"Godfuckingdammit," I say. This explains the recent surge in visitor complaints.

"They're going to fire my ass," Landry says.

Just then the light changes. The sky darkens, then turns a weird, luminous green. There's a rumble of thunder, followed by a moaning sound which at first I think is my phone on vibrate. It's not my phone.

"Did you hear that?" I say.

This time we both hear it. It's definitely moaning—human moaning. We follow the sounds to a hiker. He's sitting on a promontory with his legs outstretched in a patch of shade that's rotating in an unusual way. Judging by the earbuds in his ears, he's still transfixed by the audio tour, a narrative evocation of natural wonders and the labyrinths of time. It's keyed to the overlook, not the trail. No wonder he's in distress.

At least it's not another rainbow incident. The week before last, we afflicted a whole troop of Boy Scouts with petit mal seizures, their eager eyes staring fixedly at our vista.

When we get up close to the hiker, I realize it's worse than I thought. It's not just an audio tour malfunction, it's a viewshed disruption. He's dazed and pointing.

Out on this ledge you can see the real. It's not just Moderately Seen. It's Visible.

I remember a backpacking trip out there with one

girlfriend. She gashes her leg on some limestone, she's on the ground all quiet and I'm next to her with first aid, both of us shocked by the white inside of her. This is what we are, this flesh.

It's ugly and sullied and beautiful, the real. There's conservation, there's preservation. Does any of it matter? We don't want much, just paradise. The yearning I feel is a stab in the gut so sharp I clutch my side, and for a moment I don't breathe. It's not about wanting the perfect place. It's about wanting someone to be there with.

The hiker whimpers softly, and our training kicks in. We carry him off the ledge, remove his earbuds, get him stabilized. I've still got the passcode—they never changed it—and with a couple of keystrokes on my phone the viewshed is restored.

Landry reaches into his pack and pulls out a can of Rainier, which we share. It's only semi-cold in its neoprene sleeve, but still.

"Let's move some rocks," I say.

"What about the IMP?" Landry asks.

"Screw the IMP. We're de-maintaining this trail."

The hiker struggles to his feet. He still looks dazed, but he's taking sips from his hydration pack. Over the sound of sliding rock—a beautiful sound—he asks, "Who are you guys, anyway?"

Landry and I answer together. "We're Utah WildMall Rangers."

WONDERS OF THE WORLD

It's been snowing all day here in southeast Utah. I've been checking the road report online. It's snow-packed and icy from Moab south to the state line. I'm not going anywhere. North of here, around Monti-cello, where the winds come off the mountains, there are often drifts across 191, especially in the south-bound lane. I like the way a winter storm will turn our landscape black and white. No one comes here much at this time of year, and for a brief period it's as if our mesas and monuments are undiscovered, new and strange instead of world famous. In the late af-ternoon, when I do venture out, the air is thick with freezing fog. The streets are white and empty as I navi-gate to the grocery store for popcorn, then to the video store, where I pick up *King Kong*, the original version. It seems like a night for something I've seen before— a husband, rather than a blind date. It's dark by the time I leave the store. Across the street the marquee of the San Juan Theater is dark, too, and the shops around the intersection of Center and Main look as if they'll never open again. On a side street, someone's spinning their tires.

Back home I put in the DVD and settle in for some 1930s shimmer, all silver and satin. I remember something of the geography of Skull Island, and the scenes of terror in New York—Kong knocking an elevated train off its tracks, Kong's giant eye filling a high-rise apartment window. But I'd forgotten how the film starts. It's the Depression. Fay Wray is stealing an apple from a vendor's stand when a producer picks her up on the street. He offers her money and adventure and fame, plus the thrill of a lifetime, if she'll get on the ship with him. She says yes. She's hungry. She's got nothing to lose.

I'd seen the film in New York after college with Cooper, my boyfriend, who lived in an apartment in the West Village. After college in California, I'd gone east for a summer internship in publishing. I met Cooper, and when I wrangled another internship—six months, almost a real job—at a university press, I was happy to be able to stay in the city. I was an editorial assistant, and two days a week I also worked in order fulfillment, answering the phones and processing book orders on the simple computers we had then, monitors with ugly orange type. Cooper was in graduate school, studying business. In the evenings, we'd make dinner at Cooper's apartment, or get Chinese food delivered, and watch movies that we rented from the video store around the corner. The apartment had a view of the Empire State Building.

New York was a wonderment. I liked the city's soiled surfaces, the aging buildings that were so grimy they looked rubbed with charcoal, as if they were drawings of themselves. There was something of the West about the city, too. The rooftop water towers looked like the kind of weathered wooden structures you might see on a farm. There was a log cabin on the roof of one building. It wouldn't have surprised me if there were pigs up there, and sweet-smelling hay. Anything seemed possible on top of those buildings.

For us, too, it felt like anything was possible. On sticky summer nights, Cooper and I would walk through the endless lavender twilights, down sidewalks that were a mosaic of discarded gum and cigarettes. I was surprised and pleased to have a boyfriend in New York, one who knew the city. Cooper had grown up in the suburbs, in Connecticut. I learned the difference between Greenwich Street and Greenwich Avenue, and where to shop for vintage clothes, trying on decades like identities to avoid the awkwardness of being myself. Each weekend, Cooper and I would pick a place and head there. Bloomingdale's, the Museum of Natural History. In those days, the subway still took tokens—which are historic artifacts now. Cooper and I, when we were headed out to a restaurant or to the movies, we'd look at all the people rushing by and say, "We'd better hurry if we want a seat! Everyone's going to the same movie as us!" It was as if the whole world wanted what we wanted. We ate burgers sitting outside on noisy Seventh Avenue and slices of cake topped with extravagant chocolate curls at Café Lanciani on West Fourth. The café was near a strange little bookstore that had a basement entrance like a subway stop. The bookseller would stand outside on the sidewalk and mutter, "Books, books, want some books?" We never went down the steps. I suppose it seemed like there would be time for that someday. I hadn't yet learned what regret was, and how easy it was to avoid—to say yes.

"The best thing in the world is to be a resident tourist," Cooper would say. He had traveled as a student and had spent time in Eastern Europe. That fall, when the Berlin Wall came down, he kicked himself for not being there.

We rented *King Kong* and felt like we were in on a secret, as we looked out the window at the sliver of illumination that was the spire of the real building that Kong was clambering up in stop-motion animation on the television screen. We laughed at the corny dialogue, the producer's shipboard rehearsals— "Scream. Scream for your life!"—and his huckster showmanship. "We're millionaires, boys. Why, in a few months, it'll be up in lights on Broadway. Kong! The eighth wonder of the world!" For months afterward we talked to each other in slang from the movie. "Why, you're crazy!" and "Holy mackerel!" and "Say, why don't we…"

Cooper and I had already been seeing each other past any time frame either of us had imagined possible. A summer, then six months, and then—somehow—going on a year. "She doesn't need me." I heard Cooper say this about me, to a friend. This made me feel independent and strong. About his last girlfriend, Cooper had said, "She wanted to get married. I didn't." This made him seem much older than me, though he was only twenty-four to my twenty-two.

> > < <

On my last weekend in New York, we went to the Empire State Building—Cooper's idea. "That'd be swell!" I said. It was March, the first day of spring weather. The air was alive with warmth and softness, but out of habit we threw our winter coats on.

My internship was up. I'd applied to a program that placed teachers on Indian reservations in New Mexico and Arizona, and had been accepted, though I didn't know yet where they would send me. I was a little depressed about leaving the city. It seemed to be a narrowing of opportunities. I could no longer do anything, I would do one thing. There was a tacit agreement between Cooper and me that whatever happened—whether we'd go our separate ways, or keep seeing each other long distance—would be a decision we wouldn't force. We talked sensibly about plans, about what made sense. I didn't know then how sensible decisions, one after another, could add up to a foolish life.

We'd talked about going to the Empire State Building, and we even had a poem written about it for us, by a man who'd approached us in Washington Square Park. At first we thought he was panhandling. But he was writing verses for money.

"Any subject, any style," he said. "Pay what you want." He exuded the energy of a cartoon Tigger, enthusiastic and a little unnerving. You wouldn't have wanted him to take the seat next to you on the bus.

"The Empire State Building," Cooper said.

"Free verse," I said.

We dug into our pockets and came up with a dollar or so in change. It wasn't very much money, but on the other hand, we weren't sure that we would really get a poem.

The poet went off behind a tree, and came back ten minutes later with some lines in pencil on a sheet of paper torn from a spiral notebook. I'd been carrying it around since then, folded up in my coat pocket as a sort of talisman.

But when we got to the Empire State Building, Cooper and I fell into an argument—over the seven wonders of the world, which we were looking at in the lobby, and then about whether or not to go up to the observation deck. There were seven stained glass panels on display, one for each wonder. Cooper was sure the library at Alexandria had been one of them.

"It's not the library, it's the lighthouse," I said. We were looking right at it, luminous and gaudy. "Anyway, the line for tickets is too long."

"But we're here," Cooper said.

It wasn't that I didn't want to go to the top. I did. But going seemed to imply the end of things for us. If we didn't do it, we'd still have something to look forward to, some kind of future.

The ticket line was in the basement. Between the long, huddled wait, the endless rope line, and the accents of foreign tourists, the shabby room had the feeling of a government office. It was as if we were applying for visas to go to another country. After we'd gotten our tickets, old-fashioned blue stubs torn from a big roll, we moved into the hallway and waited some more. In line for the elevator, we leaned into each other, contrite, apologizing for the fight with our bodies. My bag slipped from my shoulder, and my feet hurt. For some reason I'd dressed for the day in a peach-colored frock and heels.

Up on the observation deck, the wind was gusting as if we were out at sea. A couple was kissing near us. I envied them their visible involvement with each other.

Cooper steered me toward the rail. I held my coat and dress down against my legs. The poem rustled in my pocket. Eighty-six stories below, traffic was flowing in the deep, intricate channels of the streets. All the individual horns and motors came together in a unified murmur that rose up to us like the sound of a river running over rocks. Straight down, and straight

ahead to the horizon, as far as we could see, the
depths and distances seemed impossibly big, Grand
Canyon big, as if only nature could have assembled a
landscape on this scale.

I imagined Cooper turning to me and telling me
in an offhand way, like Fay Wray's handsome boyfriend on the ship, "Say, I guess I love you." And if he
did, what would I say? I might protect myself a little.
"Don't get sappy on me, mister."

When I turned my attention back to the observation deck, there were hordes of people crisscrossing
the deck like bits of kaleidoscope color, and Cooper
was no longer at my side. He was gone. At any rate, I
didn't see him anywhere. I made a quick circuit around
the observation deck, trying to ignore my pinched
toes. Could he have taken the elevator down? Maybe
he thought I'd left before him. I wanted to cry—child-
ish, I know. Still searching, I cut through the gift shop
at the center of the observation deck, squeezing past
the racks of souvenir key chains and coffee mugs that
had made King Kong into a captive spokesman for the
Big Apple.

That was when I saw him: the ape himself, resplen-
dent in fake fur.

At the climax of the movie, Kong clings to the outside of the tower. He swats away the airplanes, then
drops to his death. His enormous body fills the street
below. The verdict is, "It was beauty killed the beast."
But on the observation deck that day, the beast was

happy, in his element, working the crowd. Through the fixed, comically fierce expression of the mask, human eyes peered out, lively and amused. Our eyes met. The ape lurched toward me. In the logic of my heart, I thought it was Cooper in the suit—in those days there was no one else for me—and when he opened his arms I went into them without hesitation.

The king of the apes was shorter than I expected, shaggy and soft, and he smelled of warm polyester and Aqua Velva. He grabbed me and didn't let go. In the embrace of Kong, eighth wonder of the world, I turned my head to look at the crowd and found Cooper, surprised, looking back—at me, a woman who didn't need him.

PERSUASION

h e noticed the bookmobile at the overlook one day toward the end of summer. He did the things that needed doing—tightening screws on a shade shelter, putting graphite on the lock of the restroom door where a tourist had complained of getting stuck. He did something that didn't need doing—looking northeast, beyond the wooded mesa top, toward the depths and recessions of Arch Canyon, the landscape of sandstone and shadow where someone had gone over the edge the year before. Accident or suicide, he hadn't heard which. He locked up his tools and walked over to the bookmobile, parked at the far end of the parking area.

A bookmobile used to serve the isolated communities of southeast Utah—Montezuma Creek, Bluff, Mexican Hat, Monument Valley, Oljato—but the county had gotten rid of it. This was a different vehicle: a GMC RV from the 1970s, with BOOKMOBILE stenciled on the side in faded paint.

He knocked on the door.

"It's open." A girl's voice, low and sweet.

Out of the midday glare, his eyes took a moment to adjust to the dim interior. The vehicle was lined with wooden shelves that rose from floor to ceiling, curving gracefully at the back corners. Venetian blinds shaded the windows. There was a card catalog gleaming with brass hardware, a dictionary open on a lectern, and a marble bust of someone he thought he should be able to identify.

The bookmobile girl was sitting at a small walnut desk, reading a book. She set her finger on the page to mark her place. "Can I help you find anything?" she asked.

She was wearing glasses, but she was kind of good-looking. Strands of hair had escaped her ponytail, as if the excitement of reading had left her disheveled. She wasn't that young, on second glance, but she wasn't old either. She was wearing a skirt, he noticed.

"I'm just looking around."

He skimmed the shelves. The books were mostly paperback romances, Harlequins and such. The kind of books that women liked.

"Sure I can't help you?"

He stole a glance at the librarian's ankles. "I just came in to use the Internet."

"It's over there." She pointed. "We have wireless, too."

> > < <

Fall came. Up in the mountains, the aspens turned gold. Frosty mornings made him think grimly about another long, lonely winter in town. Warm afternoons made things seem not so bad. One day, the bookmobile turned up down the road from his place. He could see it from his kitchen window: through the junipers, a stenciled letter B. The breeze through the open window set his wallpaper trembling. He hadn't noticed before that the wallpaper print resembled the floral pattern of her skirt, but flat and peeling, not in silken motion. He opened a beer. He drank half. He headed out, then went back in to brush his teeth.

Inside, the bookmobile looked different than he'd remembered it, more comfortable. A pair of old-fashioned, high-backed leather sofas sat companionably at the rear of the vehicle. The last light of the day angled in between the slats of the blinds, touching some older volumes he hadn't noticed the first time—hardcovers bound in plain cloth, with gold stamping on the spines.

The girl looked up from her book and smiled. "You came back," she said.

"Yeah." He was pleased that she remembered him. He checked his email and surfed the Internet for a while, then got up to examine the hardcovers. All of the books seemed to be by Jane Austen. Inspection revealed that they were all the same title, *Persuasion*. In the corner, a grandfather clock ticked away the minutes.

"Can I help you find something?"

"I'm just looking around."

He pulled a copy of *Persuasion* off the shelf—an old one, bound in maroon cloth. The volume fell open in his hands with a pleasing weight and an autumnal smell, like leaf mold and wood smoke. A wildflower fluttered out—a columbine, pressed flat and almost colorless. This book had been up in the mountains. He restored the flower to its place.

"What's this book about?" he asked.

She joined him by the shelves. "It's about second chances," she said. Her cheeks flushed as she told him the outline of the story: how Anne Elliott had been persuaded to refuse her suitor, Captain Wentworth, and how they met again eight years later, when they were ready to live their own lives and not the lives that others wanted for them.

She took the book from his hands. Sitting up very straight on the sofa opposite him, she read out loud:

> He was ... a remarkably fine young man, with a great deal of intelligence, spirit and brilliancy; and Anne an extremely pretty girl, with gentleness, modesty, taste, and feeling. Half the sum of attraction, on either side, might have been enough, for he had nothing to do, and she had hardly any body to love ...

He interrupted her. "I don't read fiction."

"Why not?" she asked.

He called it a waste of time, reading a made-up story when life was full of real ones.

"You watch movies, don't you?" she challenged him.

He frowned and said he didn't like novels. He added, "It's nothing personal."

The propane lamps flickered on, startling him. Suddenly he was conscious of her presence near him, and the lateness of the hour. He'd been there too long.

"Well," he said. "See you around."

At midnight he went out in the yard to pee. The bookmobile was still parked down the road, a soft glow emanating from its windows. Gaslamps and candles. The night was cold; it would be a hard freeze, the first of the season. He shivered.

Nothing to do? Wentworth had nothing on him.

> > < <

The next time he saw her was out at Muley Point. The bookmobile was backed in too close, he thought, to the edge, the big view over Goosenecks toward Monument Valley. Another suicide spot. He set some rocks behind the wheels. The tires were old and worn. He took apart an illegal fire ring and dispersed the ashes. From the rim, he studied the Goosenecks, the massive entrenched meanders, gray and blue and brown, where the San Juan River had dug its canyon a thousand feet below. A private tour van pulled up and disgorged a dozen geology enthusiasts. They peppered him with questions, and he discoursed dutifully about the formations, hoping she wouldn't leave before the group did.

The bookmobile was a pleasant refuge from the wind and the dust—but copies of *Persuasion* had spread like tumbleweed, aggressively. They were everywhere—piled helter-skelter on the shelves, stacked on the floor—not only the antique volumes, but paperbacks, beat-up copies with cracked spines reinforced with tape, well-thumbed and dog-eared textbooks with faded price stickers, and brand-new ones with glossy, unbroken backs.

"Can I help you find anything?"

It was her usual question. He tried to think of something practical, like a nature guide or a field guide. She said she didn't have anything like that.

"OK," he said. "What about self-help?"

She nodded. He watched as she unlocked a glass-front cabinet and took out a small, sturdy box that she opened like a book. "A Solander box," she said. She explained its contents: four duodecimo volumes, a first edition of *Persuasion* (John Murray, London, 1818) bound in vellum, with marbled endpapers in a peacock-feather pattern of dove gray, sky blue, and chestnut brown.

With capable, practiced movements, she arranged foam wedges on her desk to support one of the small volumes. His eyes fell on a passage:

> ...amidst the dash of other carriages, the heavy rumble of carts and drays, the bawling of newsmen, muffin-men and milkmen ... she made no complaint. No, these were noises which belonged to the winter pleasures ...

She apologized for the foxing on the pages. He wondered what she looked like under her dress.

Abruptly, he got up. "I told you I don't read novels," he said. He sounded more angry than he meant to.

The screen door banged shut behind him.

> > < <

He saw the bookmobile often after that day, but only at a distance. Pulled off on a spur road near Comb Ridge and the old highway. (He hit his brakes and reversed.) In the mountains, jolting and swaying over the narrow Causeway; she waved at him from behind the wheel. ("Who's that?" asked the girl he was with. "No one," he said. "No one.") And once he saw it up near Canyonlands, in an impossible place, on top of a sandstone dome. It was a trick of perspective; even with binoculars he couldn't see the road that must have run behind and a little above the dome.

He happened to be working near Arch Canyon when she returned to the overlook where he'd seen her first. Busy posting signs and closing some old roads, he avoided her. At the end of the week, he stopped by and said, "You can't stay here." There was a limit on camping, and she'd exceeded it.

She looked hurt, then sad, then perfectly composed as she told him she understood.

"Put some air in your tires," he told her.

He watched her drive away. The dust kicked up by the vehicle was visible as far as the highway. He knew one thing: it was easier to be alone, than to get used to being alone again.

> > < <

A few days later, a storm hit: wind and rain and hail. A microburst left tree limbs scattered in his yard. He wondered where she was riding out the storm. He worried about the vehicle. Anything might have happened: engine trouble, a falling tree, a wash-out, snow in the high country. He went out after work hours and drove the back roads, watchful for any sign of the bookmobile.

He found her on Elk Ridge, camped in a meadow. He felt relief, and then, at the sight of a pickup pulled over in the same clearing, a piercing jealousy. Some guys were talking to her—hunters, by the look of them. It was the first time he'd seen her outside. She seemed to be wearing hiking boots with her dress.

Captain Dickworth, he thought to himself. He hung back under the ponderosas until the truck pulled away and she'd gone back inside.

He tapped at the door.

"Hey," he said. "Can I check that book out?"

He stuffed a copy of *Persuasion* into his pack. That evening, in the shelter of his tent, he pulled out the book, a Penguin paperback with a painting of cottages on the cover. It was a well-worn copy, dog-eared, with underlinings and highlights in the text, and a bright yellow sticker on the spine that said USED.

He flipped through the pages. Words and phrases

met his eye: Lyme—Bath—Captain Wentworth—Anne Elliott—winter pleasures.

The bookmobile girl wasn't even his type. She was kind of pale. And kind of soft.

He turned to page one.

He would get her into shape.

A DISH OF STINGING NETTLES

hey didn't find any morels in the forest. He told her it was too early—the aspens were just starting to leaf out—and they should look for nettles instead. He said they were edible, that cooking would take the sting away. She liked the attention he paid to forest things. They were in the mountains, the Abajos, foraging near a stream. Water was running everywhere—an icy rush down the streambed, rivulets down the road. Calendar spring, snow not yet out of the question. She walked on cobbles. Those cobbles— was it a dry wash that was running or an old road that had flooded? The streambank part of the forest was boggy, almost a swamp. She tripped over water birch. She soaked her boots. She felt a flash of anger. And he was a stranger again…

She'd moved to southeast Utah for the dry places. If she hiked back out to the main road, turned around right now and hiked out, she would see the dry land laid out like a map of itself, all the ridges and the canyons, down across White Mesa and west toward the Bears Ears. Those stone unfoldings had become her everyday world and—it must be said—they'd lost a little of their old mystery and allure. Slickrock and sun-glare still pleased her, but the forest was her nature crush—a wet, dark tangle, the opposite of what she'd thought she wanted.

Besides, she'd always felt a little uneasy in the woods. It wasn't the trees so much as what the trees might be hiding. Woods brought out, magnified, all the relic fears of childhood. Grownup anxieties, too. The specter of getting lost.

Hansel and Gretel. House of bread, house made of candy and cake.

Young Goodman Brown meets the devil, and his own sweet wife.

Something curtained and concealed. She had to be careful or she'd freak herself out.

He'd asked her on this hike, yet he didn't seem to care about keeping her close. In fact, after thrusting a paper sack at her he'd proceeded to outpace her. She was left to trail after as best she could. She strained to hear the snap of a twig, a snatch of whistled melody that would confirm she was going the right way. She held her sack. She hoped there were no bears.

Catching sight of him through the trees, she hurried onward, feeling a little ridiculous; it was early in their acquaintance, this was not explicitly a date, and her actions mimicked a devotion that he hadn't earned, or asked for. At times the flash of his shirt was all she could see—a scrap of fabric like a bird hopping from branch to branch, never settling long.

Mud, stones, water. She persuaded herself of the continuation of the road.

When she finally caught up with him—a small victory—he told her that this whole time she'd been walking past patches of stinging nettles. Without the lens of language, she didn't know what they were; she'd seen only a green blur.

He knew.

He hadn't actually cooked them, himself. He'd been wanting to try it, he said.

So these were nettles. Stinging nettles.

She brushed the saw-tooth edge of a leaf, then stroked the fine hairs the way she liked to do with cactus spines, mixing caution with the need to touch. *Of course it hurts!* he teased. (Later she would look it up, and find out that nettle hairs contained a cocktail of formic acid, histamine, and serotonin. That was the combination that set her palm on fire.)

Imagine eating this.

She told him what *she* knew about the plant. It was a story: the Hans Christian Andersen tale in which a girl had to spin stinging nettles to make shirts to save her brothers. They were under a spell cast by a wicked queen: eleven boys turned into eleven wild swans. Eleven shirts of nettle cloth would turn them back.

So, in the forest, when he said they would gather stinging nettles, that they were edible, she felt the inevitability of the task: the gathering, cooking, and eating of something impossible. Trips into the forest were meant to be like that. Sling a basket over your arm, tie a red hood tight under your chin. With that daily bravery their own ancestors had gone into the dark woods of Europe, back when they were Indians.

It pleased her to tell this story—to have his attention.

It pleased her that nettles were real, and that they would cook them together. She could feel the juice, a fever in her skin.

Not impossible.

> > < <

That afternoon at his place—it is her first time inside his house—he hands her the gloves and a pair of kitchen scissors. It's her turn to work. The gloves are big, they fit loosely on her hands. In them she feels rough and capable. What she wants most of all now is to stay awhile inside this skin, these other hands. She concentrates on her work; she is an island of self. Calmly, she talks about spinning. She claims that all women possess at least one antique skill; spinning is hers.

Having told the story about spinning nettles, though, it returns to trouble her. What was so bad about being a swan? Was nettle cloth the only solution? Maybe the girl is wrong to believe that. Young, methodical, and determined, her hands swell and blister and bleed as she spins wild thread and weaves wild

cloth. The nettles buck and spit. They fight the girl.
They do not want to be cloth.

She trims the thick leaves off the stems. She chops
onion, garlic, and ginger. She sets the pan on the
stove, turns on the gas. He hands her a wooden spoon.
He says it's maple wood. She sees its wild nature. It is
only in the guise of a spoon.

EVERYWHEN

after the fire, after the phone calls and the insurance and the paperwork, Samuelsen went back to what had been his house.

House, home, whatever. The little singlewide. The smell of blackened earth, sweet as burnt sugar, brought back the southwest Colorado of his childhood—springtime, smoke curling over the fields. He parked in his usual spot, a formality now, and entered the ruins.

The living room threshold, black and twisted. The kitchen, the bathroom. It was hard to tell the roof from the floor.

The things that had meant something to him—the books, the gear, his great-grandfather's woodworking tools. The things that had just sort of accumulated, the scree slope of his life. The chain saw catalog. Five years' worth of back issues of *Mountain Gazette*. Socks.

It was all gone.

Ashes to ashes, funk to funky.

I got nothing, Samuelsen thought. The standup comic's trademark line, an easy laugh.

He walked the house room by room, respecting the floor plan. The bedroom, and the extra room at the back which he called the guest room, though as the years passed, there'd been fewer and fewer guests. He did survey. There was the incinerated and the merely charred. The fake wood and the real wood. Made in USA, made in China. His decisions of conscience, his consolations, the ways he punished himself, the museum of his life. Samuelsen: archaeologist, poet, dumbass.

He'd been away, on a trip into the mountains, and was taking the scenic route back, a long, slow drive on forest roads, when the landscape opened up and Verizon started beeping messages at him. There'd been an electrical fire, a short of some kind. It wouldn't have taken long, moving inside the walls, then the whole structure up in flames and no neighbors close enough to notice until it was too late.

He'd treated this place as temporary, even after it was paid off. There was no point in getting attached. That was what he used to tell himself, and anyone else who would listen.

He remembered a long-ago lunch break on the White Mesa dig. They'd set up their lawn chairs and mini coolers next to the PGS, the prehistoric ground surface, where a Basketmaker pit house revealed, in its carefully stacked manos, a tidy domesticity. Ashes and hearths. Each lens of ash told a story—was part of the story of the place, the big story that included, now, these spikes and pin flags, the clutter of whisk brooms and clipboards, and the construction crew blading on the other side of the fence. Someone had said to him, *You'll never settle down. You'll have girlfriends and storage units.*

That had not been entirely true.

A secondhand couch, a decent mattress. The deck and the grill. Two years ago, finally, a new canoe.

Chemistry was all he had now. This had been metal, this plastic. The grubby blue Ensolite pad he'd saved for another field season. Brown zip-up insulated Carhartt overalls—his beloved potato suit. His trowel.

Samuelsen exited through the back wall, one of the ones the firefighters had sawed through, and retreated to the truck, which was waiting, doglike, for the house to come back. He got a beer out of the cooler, popped off the cap with the opener that was fixed inside the tailgate. He drank. He opened another.

Samuelsen had nothing.

Except. From this vantage point he could see—weirdly, as if a column of superheated air had lifted it out of harm's way then set it back down on the smoke-stained edge of the bathroom sink—her toothbrush, bright nylon green and cheery as a child's toy.

When she left little things behind at his place, like her ponytail holders, he used to tease her. *Are you marking your territory?*

But he had put the toothbrush out for her.

On one of the days he didn't want to remember—

it was last winter, not even a whole year ago—he'd noticed that she'd gained weight. What happened to your stomach? Are you pregnant? He kidded her, thinking that she looked good, sexy, a little flushed from the hot shower, drops of water on her skin, her nipples standing up. And then—when she sagged into his arms, crying, not sexy anymore, just the naked unhappy weight of her—his awful realization that she wanted to be. Pregnant. But she was too old, and he'd never wanted kids, he'd told her that all along.

Samuelsen eased himself off the tailgate.

He was in the business of the prehistoric past. There were plenty of recent events that he would just as soon forget, that he was *allowed* to forget. He felt anger at the fire and the incomplete job it had done.

Reluctantly, he moved toward the spot of green.

Her toothbrush. The end had melted into a syrupy twist, but it was still quite identifiable. He'd kept a supply of cheap ones for scrubbing artifacts on bad weather days when the crew worked in the lab.

The poet in Samuelsen pondered a defect of the English language. Everything, everywhere, everyone. The plenitude. But there was no word for time's grip on his mind, the incessant reruns. There was no undoing that moment, for instance, that split second when she understood that he couldn't be what she'd thought, or hoped, he was. Everywhen. It would work, he thought, in Anglo-Saxon. A useful word if you were, say, Beowulf. First the fight, then the story of the fight.

The toothbrush in his hand had the proportions of a worked bone tool, a fine and slender type of awl, made from a mammalian long bone, commonly mule deer, split and shaped and smoothed.

He knew how to reach her. Had a number for her, anyway. But then what? He had an artifact he couldn't show her and some words he couldn't say.

RECAPTURE

ean was at Recapture Reservoir, looking for birds on the first long Sunday afternoon after the clocks changed. It had rained most of that day and the previous night. The mountains were cloud-wreathed, the lake a gothic gray, leaden and stony and unremarkable. He knew each cove and inlet, each scraggly cottonwood tree. He walked around for a while. He checked on the ruin, a couple of rooms flanked by cottonwoods, and dragged some brush over between the trees as camouflage. These boulders around the shore, their feet in water—if rocks had a consciousness, and he thought they might, what did they make of this landscape that had changed on them? He'd heard that the reservoir was meant originally to be a state park. Just as well that didn't happen. He liked it like this, without the infrastructure, the day use fee, and all the rest. He liked the little ruin, which was in plain sight from the boat ramp if you looked, but no one ever looked. Even the neglect appealed to him—the dried-out grayish edge of the shore, the graffiti on the barricade, the dumpster and

all the trash that hadn't quite made it there, the plastic bottles and disposable diapers. The unkemptness
reminded him of places he used to play, loved to play,
when he was a kid. Vacant lots, the in-between places
that nobody much cared about.

He saw the car first, then the girl, then the guy.
They were on the north side of the lake, pretty far
down the road. The car looked like a rental. It was at
an odd angle. Stuck in the mud, Dean thought.

The close-up view through binoculars: The guy, a
husband-type in khakis who did not interest him, and
the girl, who did. A veil of shiny hair, a Hopi brace-
let heavy on her wrist. The gleam of money. She was
standing on the road, a disgusted distance away from
the mud-spattered vehicle. The guy got into the car.
Her posture was helpless, defiant. She'd been driving
and they were stuck and it was her fault. Dean waited
to see if they could get out of it. This was better than
birds.

The sound of the wheels spinning carried across
the lake.

The sky brightened, a white glare. The girl shaded
her eyes with her hand. She seemed to be looking
across the lake straight at Dean, like she was saying
What are you waiting for?

He took his time. Got back in the truck, lumbered
out on the access road then onto the highway north
across the dam. What were they doing out here? The
road on the north side of the lake was slick, with

patches of boggy mud. He steered expertly, showing them how it was done.

When he got out of the truck, he was surprised to see that she was a tall girl. In heels she'd be taller than he was. Khaki shorts were not boring on her. She looked like Jane in an old Tarzan movie, star of her own safari.

"Hey," he said.

"Hey."

"Are you stuck?"

She looked at him incredulously. The car was a little Ford, almost certainly a rental, with Utah plates—the orange of Delicate Arch visible through the mud.

The husband, behind the wheel, rolled the window down. "She thought we'd be able to turn around here."

Dean heard the put-down. She did, too, and didn't like it. Their eyes met. In that instant, he knew she'd seen him across the lake, she'd seen the binoculars—some telltale glint.

"Let her drive," Dean said.

Dean and the husband got behind the vehicle, Dean on the driver's side. Dean shouted, "Give it some gas!"

The difference between stuck and unstuck: three people instead of two. What were they doing out here, anyway?

The husband, back in charge now, said to Dean, "Looks like we owe you some thanks."

"That's not necessary," Dean said, before the guy

could reach for his wallet.

There were introductions, the kind that Dean always found unnecessary. He wasn't going to see these people, Walter and Kelsey, again.

"Can we at least buy you a drink?" the girl, Kelsey, asked.

"In Blanding?" He laughed.

"Wait a second." She walked to the water's edge— it had been ice just a week or two ago. There were some sherds on the little beach, scattered fragments of gray ware, a few of them under the water. She picked one up.

"Walter, look at this."

A look passed between her and the guy, some excitement.

"We need to get going, babe."

"Isn't there any place for a drink?" She said this to Dean. "Or lunch. What about lunch?"

"There's no place," Dean said. He looked back toward the highway, avoiding her gaze. Welcome to Blanding. They'd been stuck in the mud, but they were out of it now, and could go back wherever they came from, back to the land of expensive haircuts.

He saw her a couple of days later at the Shell station in town. She was by herself, pumping gas.

"Hey," he said, from his truck.

Instantly her mask went up—cue the strange-man alert. Then just as quickly the mask came off and she was smiling and saying, "Oh, it's *you*."

"You're still in town," he said. Obvious statements were the safest, he'd found, when it came to women.

"For awhile," she said.

"Is that offer still good?"

"What?"

"Lunch?" he said. "It's lunchtime." That was why *he* was there.

She looked reflexively at her watch. "Why not?"

Ten minutes later they were sitting at a molded plastic table-and-bench in the gas station's taco annex. She'd ordered a diet soda, while he'd gone all out with a burger and fries.

"Where's your husband today?" he asked.

"He had to go back to work," she said. "He's not my husband."

She'd dropped him off at the airport in Moab the day before. An expensive ticket.

Kelsey was staying in town—also for work. "Research," she clarified. She took something out of her tote and handed it across the table. An old photo postcard, sepia-toned, cracked inside its plastic sleeve.

He studied the picture, taken somewhere around the turn of the century he guessed: a cliff dwelling, tucked like a swallow's nest into a long, low alcove, a tidy row of buildings with a tower at one end. UTAH was hand-lettered in white at the bottom right corner. On the smudged and grimy back of the card, the word *chimney* was scrawled in pencil in a loopy cursive that reminded him of his grandmother's handwriting.

She was looking at him expectantly.

He shrugged.

"That's Recapture Ruin," she said. "Have you heard of it?"

"No." Ruins like this were a dime a dozen in this part of Utah, he told her.

"When we saw the sign for Recapture Recreation Area, we were hoping it would have been back in those cliffs. That's why we pulled over, to have a look."

"This isn't by the lake." He was sure of that.

"What if it's flooded—somewhere under all that water. Those potsherds …"

"There's Recapture Reservoir. There's Recapture Canyon, too. And Chimney Wash." He tapped the back of the card, handed it back to her. "Maybe this is Chimney Wash, I don't know."

"You know a lot of places," she said, impressed.

He waved off the compliment.

"Really!" she said. "I told Walter, we should have asked you about the site when we were at the lake. He didn't want me to mention it. Anyway, *I* could use a guide. Someone who knows the area."

"Yeah," he said, "since you don't know what you're doing. You'll get hopelessly lost. Or stuck."

"I did fuck up the rental car," she admitted. "What about you? Would you be interested?"

"I don't think so." He looked out at the gas pumps. It was getting busy—the spring tourist season.

She reached into her bag and, with no fumbling—

he liked that, he had no patience for women who carried too much shit around—she found a business card. "Call me if you change your mind."

Under Kelsey's name, the card said "Experience Design." (Whatever that was. Dean had a vision of her in her other life, her real life, walking fast through some glass cathedral of a lobby, with takeout coffee in her hand.) Under that she wrote the name of her motel, and her room number.

He was not going to change his mind. She was too pretty, and her not-husband was too conveniently absent.

He walked out to his truck, digesting the conversation, and then went back in with a handful of maps. The one she had was useless. She was still sitting at the table, looking out the window at something only she could see. "Here. Take these."

"Thanks!" she said, meaning it.

He pointed out where Recapture Canyon ran down toward Chimney Wash.

"X marks the spot?" she said.

> > < <

She traced the canyon with her index finger after he left. Recapture Canyon, Chimney Wash. Walter had handed her this project after he'd taken her on the special trip, just the two of them, almost a year ago. Some Santa Fe spa time, then up to Colorado and Mesa Verde National Park. The whole time he'd seemed to be brimming with excitement, something he was keeping back from her. At the time, she'd been afraid he was going to propose. She'd have had a hard time turning down an offer like that. At Cliff Palace they followed the ranger through the gate, down the CCC steps, and stood around in the freezing cold at seven thousand feet, allegedly spring. Then, back in California, they drove a long, long way out past Barstow—she remembered being disgruntled in a gas station restroom in Newberry Springs—to a place off old Route 66, Walter's family's decaying property, a sort of dude ranch from the Roy Rogers days. And back in the cliffs…

She scrambled up into the ruin, delighted. It was beautiful and strange: *Sunset Boulevard* meets the National Park Service. The cliff dwelling resembled the small sites she'd seen at Mesa Verde: miniature, enchanted in the late afternoon light. Later, she thought how wrong it was that the ruin was there. Up close you could see how the stones were held together with concrete, patched together, not always with skill. But that came later, the ruefulness and the problem of undoing what should never have been done. First came delight.

"I want you to research this," Walter told her. Because, it turned out, the ruin was a problem for him, or could be. He donated to environmental causes, and there were business dealings that this property could complicate as well. It had to do with water, with the tribes and the casinos. She didn't follow all the ins and outs. What it came down to was that it didn't look good, having this ruin.

She needed to find the site and Dean, she thought, was just the person to help.

> > < <

Dean drove down to Chimney Wash, telling himself he would just take a look around. He'd been there before, once, but it had been a long time. East of Bluff he turned off the highway to Montezuma Creek, turned again, then had to consult the gazetteer. After a long, bumpy drive he came to the towers. There were two of them, connected by a series of rooms collapsed into rubble, and they stood at the head of a canyon, a windswept and dusty place. People came out here, though. The place was all tracked up, and you could drive right up to the site. This had been someone's home. People had been content here, presumably. He prowled around below the site for a while, looking down into the wash where the chimneys stood—they looked a little like the Navajo Twins in Bluff, and a little Egyptian, like some time-eroded monument. He drove around some more, keeping an eye out for the girl's—Kelsey's—ruin.

It could have been anywhere. It could be nowhere—collapsed, pothunted.

At the mill that week, Dean was working with contractors, a crew from California full of complaints—the food, the motels, the wind and the dust. They were lonely and bored, they hated being in Blanding.

All day Dean shouted and was shouted at over the grating roar of the excavators. On the other side of the orange fencing, the archaeologists were scurrying with their buckets of dirt. He knew exactly what they were finding. Sherds and lithics, lithics and sherds. No surprises there, he was sure, but it was work and it had to be done. There were girls on this archaeology crew—in principle that was a plus, though they were dressed like the guys in Carhartt from their shoulders down to their ankles, so in practice it made no difference at all. Skinny girls and skinny guys. Young, too— most of them looked no more than a year or two out of school. Leaving the site at the end of the day, Dean drove past the cell, where the decoy bald eagle didn't fool the ducks often enough. A gust of wind blew yellow spray toward his vehicle. He got the window up just in time.

This was his life.

Driving back into town one evening, he saw her car in the motel lot amongst all the contractor pickups. The motel sign was flashing with the sickly glow of aging neon. He went home, showered, washed the day off his body, and had the unpleasant feeling there was not much left of him.

When he knocked he could feel her looking through the peephole, her fisheye view of him. That was how he felt, all eyes and mouth, all the wanting parts.

She opened the door. The TV was on, tuned to the

Weather Channel—suns and clouds and the idiotic tune that accompanied the local forecast. She had a manila folder in her hand, and there were more files arranged in neat stacks on the dresser and the small desk.

"You're working," he said.

"Obsessively," she said. "I should stop."

Which one of them started it? He was walking her over to the bed, it was his doing, but she was letting him, she still had the folder in her hand and was reaching for a safe place to put it.

"We should stop," he said. Her words in his mouth. He knew they wouldn't, though.

She was young, her confidence turning into uncertainty in bed. She didn't know what she wanted, wasn't quite at ease in her body. That was OK, he knew what he wanted. This was what he'd been looking for when he drove out to Recapture that lonesome Sunday, and he hadn't even known it. He'd wanted this beating heart, this body. It could have been anyone, it happened to be her. To his relief, there was no tenderness, no declaration of feelings. She earned his undying gratitude for that.

But then she was out of bed and back in her clothes in the most matter-of-fact way, and in spite of himself he was miffed.

"What are you doing?" he asked. "Are you going somewhere?"

"I want to show you something."

She turned on the bedside lamp—he flinched at the glare—clicked her phone on and tilted the little screen so he could see the image. It was the ruin on the postcard, a little more crumbled, part of the tower gone, but clearly the same place.

"I told you I don't know where it is," he said.

"I do. It's in California. I'm not looking for the ruin," she said. "I'm looking for the site."

It had happened in the 1890s. A wealthy family on a tour of the Southwest, passing through southeast Utah, saw the cliff dwelling and took action to save it from looters. It was labeled piece by piece, dismantled, loaded onto wagons, then shipped by train from Flagstaff to Barstow.

"Are you serious?"

She'd told this story before. It was a story that she told, not a story for him in particular. Reconstructed in California, it opened to visitors in 1900, six years before the Antiquities Act. It was in the Mojave Desert, somewhere between Barstow and Needles— Dean gathered that she didn't want to say too much about the location.

He leafed through a folder of photocopies, reproductions of old photographs. A cliff dwelling, walls and kivas and a two-story tower, women in long skirts and big hats in front of it and a little girl perched on a wall, an expedition. Along the bottom of the cliff a row of date palms—the trees weren't there anymore, she said.

"Like Scotty's Castle," he said, thinking of the estate near Death Valley. The kind of private playground that used to exist, dude ranches and Roman plunge pools.

She'd done her research, as much as she could, and hit a brick wall. She'd gone to the Bancroft Library at Berkeley, and the Denver Public Library. She had requests out to museums and archives, for photos, maps, sketches—anything at all that would help to relocate the original site of the ruin. It was possible that it had simply not been documented.

The ruin had served as the location for a handful of silent films, none surviving, including *The Cliff Dwellers*, a Romeo and Juliet set in the prehistoric Southwest. In its heyday in the 1930s, the house on the property was a Hollywood party site, a second-rate Hearst mansion. Newspaper clippings showed a famous cowboys and Indians party, with Salvador Dali as the guest of honor. The Recapture Cliff Dwellings were a tourist attraction in the 1940s and 1950s—she had brochures, a copy of a billboard photo, the usual souvenir crap, some of it old, Made in Japan. And then there was the long decline, until it closed its doors in the early '70s.

"That's crazy," Dean said.

"I know!" she said. "But it's all completely authentic. It was stabilized—is that the right term?"

He said, "It's not authentic." He reached for his pants.

"OK, OK," she said. "Anyway, it's something worth preserving and we want to find out where it came from."

She didn't like arguments. That was information, that was something for Dean to learn.

"This site," he said. "What do you care?"

She said, "I sort of own it."

"Oh?"

This turned out to be not strictly true; the property was Walter's. They were more or less engaged, she said.

Dean didn't know what to say to that. Found himself disappointed, flummoxed anyway.

He reminded himself, *This doesn't involve you.*

Then he said, "We could go out there. To Chimney Wash. If you want."

> > < <

Of course she said yes. They made plans to meet that Saturday at the Shirttail convenience store, south of Blanding where Highway 95 met 191. She wrote down his directions, though it turned out there was nothing to it. It was a straight shot south of town. She parked around the back side of the store and waited. She looked at the HAY sign and the view of the mountains. It was going to be hot. A dry wind was blowing. Earthquake weather was what they called it in California. When his truck pulled in, she was careful not to look too thrilled to see him. Men didn't like that.

"Why'd you wear that?" he asked. He sounded annoyed. Good, that made her job easier.

She looked down at her skirt. "I thought it would look cute in a picture."

He said, "Wear some shorts next time. Or a skort. Girls like skorts."

"How do you know what a skort is?"

"I have a daughter."

That was unexpected.

In his truck, she felt the close-quarters discomfort, the intimacy of riding in vehicles with men you didn't know well. Accepting rides from strangers, the only way in life anything ever happened.

Though why this drive should feel more awkward than being in bed was beyond her. Maybe it was being clothed after having unclothed each other. You could never go back to before, when you didn't know what it was like. He was attractive, though. She hadn't really seen it before, not consciously. But something had made it happen. *It*.

She pulled out a tube of sunblock and dabbed it conscientiously on face, neck, ears, forearms, the back of her hands.

Out of nowhere he said, "Kelsey."

"Yeah?"

"I was just going to say—have you seen those Kelsey guides? The canyon hiking guides? That's what I think of when I say your name."

"It's a family name. It's my middle name."

He eased up on the gas, letting the wind blow a tumbleweed across the road in front of them.

"Be careful of those when you're driving," he said. "I knew someone who hit a tumbleweed. The tumbleweed hit *him*. It punctured the radiator."

"You're kidding!" she said.

"They're from the Ukraine. Tumbleweeds."

"Really? They're not American? I didn't know that."

There was so much she didn't know. She tried to take it all in. They were off the highway now. She jotted directions in a pocket spiral notebook for when she came back—she was sure she would be back—and the first couple of turns were easy but after that, one dirt track wandered into another. It wasn't one of the beautiful red rock canyons; it was more on the yellow to brown spectrum, something you'd drive past on the way to someplace more scenic. She tried to pay attention to landmarks, snapped some photos. At least things had dried out. This road would be a nightmare when wet.

She gave conversation another try. "You have a daughter?"

"Yeah."

Her prodding yielded little more. The marriage, the divorce, his work at the uranium mill. He was from California, too, which surprised her.

"Long story short," he said.

"I'd like to hear the short story long," she said.

"You got divorced?"

"Yeah. She couldn't take it."

"You, or Blanding?"

"Both."

There was a long stretch across bare rock. Dean knew where he was going. They picked up vehicle tracks on the other side.

Beyond the tower site, he parked near an old cowboy camp, a cabin made out of what was obviously reused pueblo building stone. The ground around it was strewn with old cans, thin as paper, a few bottles, and strips of tar paper. In the near distance, a long low ridge with several alcoves looked promising. But when she compared it to the photocopies she'd brought, she got frustrated. There wasn't enough background in any of the photos. They were too close up, or too washed out, hazy. Pictures of forgotten information.

With a motorized grumble, a family group roared toward them—where on earth could they have come from?—parents and kids on ATVs, teenagers on dirt bikes, helmeted and clad like superheroes in their ballistic riding gear. They split into two groups on either side of Dean and Kelsey, splitting like a herd of antelope. They knew where they were going.

"Ah, shit," she said. "I don't know what to do. I don't know where to look."

"Let's just hike," he said.

She followed him up the wash toward the base of the ridge. They climbed a low ledge, followed that, went up another level to where a small granary sat, serene and empty.

"Oh, it's lovely!" she exclaimed.

It *was* lovely, though beyond it was a creepy modern camp—tarps and a sleeping bag lying there, corpselike and mildewed. The place felt recently lived in, maybe still occupied, by the kind of person who couldn't live in town. In the old explorers' accounts, they described cliff dwellings as feeling as if the ancient people had just walked away, that the boundary between past and present was porous. Was that really a good thing? It must have creeped them out once in a while, finding corn in the ancient granaries, bowls of food in the rooms.

She slipped on loose rock and had to catch herself; she had to pay attention. The hike was exhausting and exhilarating and nothing like Mesa Verde National Park. Walter would have hated it. He liked his conveniences. Near the top of the knoll or butte or mesa, whatever it was, she sagged into the shade of a tenacious juniper that was growing out of a cleft in the rock.

"I need a break! I'm sorry," she said. The heat was killing her. She was used to sea level. What was the elevation here, five thousand feet? Also, there were gnats, against which there seemed to be no defense. She swatted at them, resigned herself to getting bitten.

Dean lay back in the dirt, comfortably.

"What will you do if you find the site?" he asked.

"I don't know." She heard herself, for the first time, sounding skeptical. "Walter wants to move it back, reconstruct it here."

Dean snorted, dismissive laughter. "It'll never happen."

"Sure it could," she said. "Don't be so negative. I'm a project manager, it's what I do." Saying it, she realized how crazy it sounded. But no more so than the original move.

If they could build an island in the shape of a palm tree, she could bring Recapture Ruin back home.

He said, "Well you won't make this happen, not a chance. The BLM won't want it."

She admitted that the BLM wasn't returning her calls. "I can't get anyone to talk to me," she said. "Walter just wants to do the right thing. God, I'm thirsty." She swigged water, wished she'd brought more. "We're going to die out here! You go on without me." He didn't play along. They were keeping their distance today. It was a vacation fling—a one-night, nothing more.

"Why are you doing this, anyway?" he asked.

"I told you," she said. "It's Walter's property, his business."

The red ridge in the distance, the blue mountains, a light wind riffling through the big sagebrush.

"Can I tell you a story?" she asked.

"Can I stop you?"

"No." Maybe the heat was what brought the story out of her. A few months ago, she'd been in Norway, an entirely different place from this. The contrast between the two places was important to the story, she thought, specifically the colors. Utah browns, mauves, reds, under a blazing blue sky. Norway in winter was the white of the snow and the fog, the water in Grimstad harbor an iridescent, steel blue. She didn't attach any emotions to these colors. They were a shortcut to convey the sense of totally different worlds. She'd gone to Grimstad to trace her family history. She wanted to know who she was, where she'd come from, ancestrally speaking. She and her second cousin Torfinn had followed a young man at Fjære kirke into the churchyard. The young man was toting a shovel—very Yorick, though the shovel was only for snow. He uncovered the gravestones she was looking for, the burial place of her great-great-grandparents Aanon Aanonsen and Theodine Marie Tobiasdatter. And then Torfinn, good-natured and full of enthusiasm, drove her around looking for the family farm. She'd brought a handful of photos of houses with her on the trip, snapshots sent from Norway to America between the 1920s and the 1940s. On the back of one was written: *vårt hus!* Our house! But whose? They'd written it with such confidence, such an absence of information for Kelsey. They knew who they were. No one remembered them now. Maybe—she thought, as Torfinn turned down yet another snow-packed country road, a world of white houses and white fields, everything disorientingly white except for the occasional fat frost-rimed horse pawing for grass under the snow—maybe it didn't matter. It was a landscape of lost memory. They stopped at several houses and talked to several women who all looked potentially like relatives with their sandy brown hair and their chins so much like Kelsey's own. Curiously, at each of these houses, hanging near the door was an old photograph or a painting of the way the house used to look. It was a very house-conscious place, Norway. But eventually they had to give up.

The next day, she took the bus from Grimstad to Kristiansand and the bus and train station there. The bus was late. She ran across the slush-filled parking lot to the platform, where two trains were closing their doors. She asked in Norwegian which train to take. The conductor waved her aboard, directing her to change at Nordagutu. The train was full of teenage girls, tall and strong with high, girlish voices. They must have been speaking New Norwegian; she couldn't understand a word except for *ikkje*—not.

It was dark when the train pulled in at Nordagutu. Kelsey pulled her rolling bag down the platform, stopping every few steps to kick away the snow that was plowing in front of it. By the time she got to the station building—there was a lot of snow to kick—the other passengers who had gotten off with her were gone. There was one car left in the parking lot. The older couple standing by it looked at Kelsey, but she wasn't the one they were waiting for. They'd caught her eye, though, and she thought she'd confused them by looking back at them so searchingly. They must have been waiting for a friend or relative who'd missed the train in Kristiansand. In that moment, it was as if all three of them were thinking: *I know you're not the one I'm looking for, but it's cold and it's dark and we'd be willing to pretend, just so we can get out of here and go home.*

When they drove away, she was alone on the platform. The light from the little wooden station gave a blue cast to the night, snow, and woods. It felt like a stage set for an Ibsen production: *Winter, Norway.*

Inside, a couple of kids sprawled on benches, dressed in black, headphones on; they glanced at Kelsey in utter boredom. She went to the counter and in Norwegian—her Norwegian was quite good that day—she asked for a ticket to Skien. The stationmaster told her she should buy the ticket on the train... *On the train*, she repeated, for the pleasure of speaking Norwegian. *Flott!* Great!

The train, when it arrived, was a tiny one—two cars, like a kids' ride at an amusement park. It had started to snow again, a gentle snow that hardly seemed cold at all. After a while, it seemed to be snowing inside the train car, too. If that's even possible, she said to Dean.

"It's possible," he said. "I've been camping when it

snowed inside my tent, from the condensation."

Besides her luggage, she had a plastic bag from the Norli bookstore in Grimstad, holding odds and ends—something to read, and some souvenirs she'd bought, including some Christmas ornaments made of straw. They're traditional, she told Dean. It was an old custom: at Christmas you slept on straw on the floor, because that was the night the ancestors returned to sleep in their own beds. That was in the old days, when they knew which house to go back to. She had a bite of a Freia chocolate bar and made it through a paragraph or two of her Norwegian crime novel before dozing off in the little train car floating through the snow. When she opened her eyes, there was a young woman sitting across from her. Unlike the bored boys with their headphones, she was looking at Kelsey, staring in fact, and unlike the couple on the platform, she didn't turn away. She looked so familiar. Kelsey got out her laptop and opened up some photo files.

Just as she thought—it was Theodine Marie Tobiasdatter, her great-great-grandmother, who had followed her from Grimstad to Nordagutu. She died at forty-two, in 1918, probably of the Spanish flu. She'd had twelve children. But on the train she was the young woman of the photo, which was taken before her marriage. She wore a feathered cap in her hair, and had a saucy tilt to her head. It was a studio portrait with a backdrop of woods and a forest path.

"Do you mean you saw a ghost?" Dean asked.

"A ghost?" Kelsey thought for a moment. "I really can't say. I mean, I don't believe in ghosts. But I'd gone looking for her, and she found me. I think she came with me because she wanted to know where I was going. I think she was curious. I mean, she never got to go to America."

She looked at Dean, thinking about the bargains people made. *I know you're not the one, but I'd be willing to pretend, just so we can sit here like this, watching the tumbleweeds and telling stories.*

Back at the motel, she said, "Thanks for the hike." She was tired, dirty, itching from gnat bites, and the day, she felt, had been a failure. She would never find the site. She had told that ridiculous story.

And then Dean was following her into the room, the plain, ugly room that disappeared when they were in bed, she couldn't see any of it, she couldn't even see him. All she could do was feel.

> > < <

She left the next morning. Back to California, back to noise and traffic and meetings, haircuts and manicures. Weeks turned into months, a semblance of work and life, not without complications. The thing with Dean—it was just something that happened. It was something she was supposed to forget. But how, exactly, to accomplish this? That second night with him, something inane on the television, Dean went to get ice, then came back with ice, and there was the understanding between them again, the conspiracy of desire. The force of it like the wind slamming a door. They were accomplices.

Was the door open or shut?

She had to find out.

One night in September she packed a bag and drove out to the desert for, she told Walter, a long weekend. The old RECAPTURE sign on the highway was sandblasted to the point of unreadability, though you could still see the arrow inviting passersby to turn for the cliff dwellings. The old ranch house was sadly dilapidated. Hiking the short trail up into the cliffs felt like walking back into Utah. They'd chosen a good location, here, if not an authentic one. At the ruin, she spread out her Thermarest and sleeping bag in the largest of the rooms. Waiting for night to fall, she walked the site, touching the buildings stone by stone and picking at the seams of the concrete or whatever it was they'd used in the reconstruction. It came away in scabby handfuls. She loosened a stone from the top course of one of the walls, held it in her hand, replaced it with a feeling of futility.

In the middle of the night, sleepless, she moved out to the plaza.

Walter could not make Recapture go away. She would not make it go away for him, for his benefit.

The next day she drove straight through to Utah. She took the cutoff to Hovenweep—she wasn't ready for Blanding yet—and camped, going on to Mesa Verde after that. The park ruins seemed sterile and well-kept. It looked too good, like they sent a cleaning crew in to vacuum the sites at night. In Cortez for an oil change, she watched the Weather Channel, sipped vile coffee that smelled of Styrofoam and tires.

Back at Recapture Reservoir, she sat by the lake. The low sandstone cliffs behind her felt cozy and protective, and the sound of water coming to shore had something companionable in it, lapping and murmuring. The voice of the lake, the raucous quacking of ducks—a world of sound that quieted the chatter in her head. She walked the lakeshore, taking it all in: the ragged stalks and stems of the plants at the water's edge, the saurian imprint of turkey tracks in dried mud, a black and ashy fire ring. Also bottle caps, broken glass, a Pepsi can, a gray ware sherd, and something that looked like white weathered bone, fragile, a cow pelvis, but it was only a plastic bag. Then another sherd.

The trail of sherds led to a little ruin guarded by cottonwood trees, just a few yards back from the lake. Of course, there had been no lake here then. It was small, a couple of rooms open to the sky. The few courses of stones were enough to lead her eye to the right angles, the walls and corners. An ordinary little place. She was inordinately pleased to have found it. She had been here before. In that spot across the lake, she'd gotten the rental car stuck. She'd been someone else then, someone who would not have discovered this ruin. Would have seen brush and leaves and dirt.

How easy it was, in the end, to let go: to get the banker's box of files out of the car, walk up the boat ramp to the little blue dumpster, tip it all in. The notes, the photocopies. Originals too, for what it was worth. She should have recycled the paper, but she wanted the stuff gone. Burning it would have been best, but she was reluctant to start a fire in this dry place.

She would tell Walter the site was under the lake.

The water was very blue, the cottonwood leaves a deep, rich gold. She took off her shoes, pushed her fingers and toes into the sand. It was fine sand, here in this spot where sand-colored boulders sheltered a little beach, with an area of gin-clear water just offshore, in the direction of the Abajos, framed between two prominent areas of rimrock. The water gleamed and glittered in the low autumn sun. For a moment, the reflection of the cliffs and the boulders on the shore looked like a cliff dwelling there under the water. And then the breeze ruffled the surface of the lake. The image vanished. She saw only what was there.

> > < <

That fall had brought a series of strange events to southeast Utah. There was the day the phones and ATMs didn't work. When you picked up the phone, you got nothing but rapid beeps, the all-circuits-are-busy-please-try-your-call-later kind. Over in Colorado, the sheriff had shot a Ute named Posey, a rerun of a headline from 1923. A few days later, at the laundromat, people were talking about the meteor that had streaked across the sky a few nights before. At least, some people said it was a meteor. Others thought it was a UFO, and still others were sure that it was an iridium flare. Whatever it was, the light was observed traveling south to north, vanishing somewhere between the reservoirs and the mountains. On that point, everyone agreed.

At the laundromat, Dean was loading wet clothes into the dryer when his attention was caught by an attractive girl by the vending machine, wearing Bermuda shorts, with a little backpack on.

The girl turned around. He recognized Kelsey. Seeing her in town was like seeing a new house on what used to be an unbuilt lot, an unsettling turn of events. She was a good-looking girl, but the fact that it was Kelsey and not a stranger was a disappointment. It was like she'd cheated him of something.

"How come you didn't call me?" he demanded.

She looked distinctly unconfident. "You never gave me your number," she said.

"I didn't think I'd see you again." He remembered how she looked in a skirt. He didn't care for those shorts.

"I didn't think I'd see *you* again," she said.

He shoved his jeans, a tangle of wet denim, into the dryer. Socks, underwear, quarters and a turn of the dial.

"What's happening with your project?" he asked.

Was she going to cry? "It's over," she said. "It'll fall

down when the Big One hits. Or maybe they'll reopen it as an attraction. I don't know. I've left Walter."

Three days later, they were driving out of town, if not exactly together, at least in the same vehicle, loaded up with the alarming amount of gear that camping seemed to require. They turned at Shirttail, headed west on 95. Kelsey slumped in the seat, shading her face with her hand. Dean liked this: the moment you got out of town, left it all behind. They flew through the roadcut, and on the other side of Comb Ridge was the reliable big view, satisfyingly geologically complex, and empty—though that was an illusion: there was almost always someone down in the wash, camped south of the highway under the cottonwoods, or over on the Arch Canyon side. It wasn't empty in the old days either, the days of sherds and lithics.

They would go camping, Dean thought, and maybe next weekend they would get some firewood. Winter was coming. They would need a lot of wood.

Kelsey was talking about the meteor, which she had seen. "Wouldn't it be weird," she said, "if aliens invaded? And took this land? We'd be the Indians then."

ACKNOWLEDGMENTS

I would like to thank the Jentel Artist Residency Program, the Center for Land Use Interpretation, the Wisconsin Institute for Creative Writing, and the Ucross Foundation for their support of my writing. Thank you, also, to the editors of the journals in which some of these stories first appeared, particularly Howard Junker of *ZYZZYVA* and Charles Finn of *High Desert Journal*; and to Mark Bailey and Kirsten Johanna Allen of Torrey House Press, who were instrumental in transforming these stories into a book.

Additional, heartfelt acknowledgments to my family, for their love and support; for advice and inspiration, Sheila Black, Rachel Gallagher, Andrew Goodwin, Jay Stevens, and Kim Todd; Glenn Kurtz, for a lifetime of encouragement; Carole Graham and Deborah Kelley-Galin, fellow contractors in curation at the Anasazi Heritage Center, for invaluable moral support (go Team DAP!); friends and colleagues at Abajo Archaeology; Ylva Bergström; Kate Keady Hoffhine; Deborah Hunt and Wayne Day of Hunt's Trading Post; Stacey Meeks; Geoff Thompson, for the petrified hoopla; photographer Michael Troutman; and Kelly Wahl. Finally, this book would not exist without the time I spent working at Edge of the Cedars State Park Museum in 2007 and 2009–10.

ERICA OLSEN

Erica Olsen lives in the Four Corners area, where she does archives and curation work for archaeology museums. A graduate of Stanford, Harvard, and the University of Montana MFA program, she has also been a Djerassi Fiction Fellow at the University of Wisconsin. Her short fiction has appeared in *ZYZZYVA*, *High Desert Journal*, and other publications, and her nonfiction pieces in magazines including *Fine Books & Collections* and *High Country News*. Her work has received awards including the 2011 Barthelme Prize for Short Prose (for "Grand Canyon II," included in *Recapture*).

About Torrey House Press

The economy is a wholly owned subsidiary of the environment, not the other way around.

— Senator Gaylord Nelson, founder of Earth Day

Headquartered in Torrey, Utah, Torrey House Press is an independent book publisher of literary fiction and creative nonfiction about the environment, people, cultures, and resource management issues of the Colorado Plateau and the American West. Our mission is to increase awareness of and appreciation for the transcendent possibilities of Western land, particularly land in its natural state, through the power of pen and story.

2% for the West is a trademark of Torrey House Press designating that two percent of Torrey House Press sales are donated to a select group of not-for-profit environmental organizations in the West and used to create a scholarship available to upcoming writers at colleges throughout the West.

Torrey House Press
http://torreyhouse.com

Also available from Torrey House Press

Crooked Creek by Maximilian Werner

Sara and Preston, along with Sara's little brother Jasper, must flee Arizona when Sara's family runs afoul of American Indian artifact hunters. Sara, Preston, and Jasper ride into the Heber Valley of Utah seeking shelter and support from Sara's uncle, but they soon learn that life in the valley is not as it appears and that they cannot escape the burden of memory or the crimes of the past. Resonating with the work of such authors as Cormac McCarthy and Wallace Stegner, *Crooked Creek* is a warning to us all that we will live or die by virtue of the stories we tell about ourselves, the Earth, and our true place within the web of life.

The Scholar of Moab by Steven L. Peck

A mysterious redactor finds the journals of Hyrum Thayne, a high-school dropout and wannabe scholar, who manages to wreak havoc among townspeople who are convinced he can save them from a band of mythic Book of Mormon thugs and Communists. Though he never admits it, the married Hyrum charms a sensitive poet claiming that aliens abducted her baby (is it Hyrum's?) and philosophizes with Oxford-trained conjoined twins who appear to us as a two-headed cowboy. Peck's hilarious novel considers questions of consciousness and contingency, and the very way humans structure meaning.

Also available from Torrey House Press

The Plume Hunter by Renée Thompson

A moving story of conflict, friendship, and love, *The Plume Hunter* follows the life of Fin McFaddin, a late-nineteenth century Oregon outdoorsman who takes to plume hunting—killing birds to collect feathers for women's hats—to support his widowed mother. In 1885, more than five million birds were killed in the United States for the millinery industry, prompting the formation of the Audubon Society. The novel brings to life an era of our country's natural history seldom explored in fiction as Fin and his lifelong friends struggle to adapt to society's changing mores.

Tributary by Barbara K. Richardson

Willa Cather and Sandra Dallas resonate in Richardson's fearless portrait of 1870s Mormon Utah. This smart and lively novel tracks the extraordinary life of one woman who dares resist communal salvation in order to find her own. Clair Martin's dauntless search for self leads her from the domination of Mormon polygamy to the chaos of Reconstruction Dixie and back to Utah where she learns from Shoshone Indian ways how to take her place, at last, in the land she loves.